COUNTEI

Tracy Lawson

COUNTERACT

© 2014 Tracy Lawson

Original Cover Artwork by Natasha Makley Strom
Cover Design by EbookLaunch.com

First Print 2014
Second Print 2015
Third Print 2016

978-1-948543-34-7

DysCovered Publishing
TracyLawsonBooks.com

To Bob, who sticks with me through every plot twist,
and to my Verbs:
Keri, the most intriguing character I ever created,
and Chase, who asked the right question

To Christian

Never take your freedoms
for granted!

COUNTERACT

So great to meet you!
Keep writing.

Tracy Lawson

Chapter 1

9:10 AM
Day 1: Friday, October 27, 2034
Quadrant OP-439 (formerly suburban Columbus, Ohio)

Careen Catecher was just a few steps from the front door of the history building when a wave of panicked students poured out, driving her back into the quad. Someone's backpack knocked her coffee mug out of her hand, and a guy she didn't know grabbed her roughly by the elbow and spun her around without breaking stride, dragging her with him as he ran. "Come on! Didn't you hear? We're supposed to go to the Student Center."

"Why? What's happening?"

The first wail of the disaster siren drowned out his answer, and she cringed as they fled across campus in the growing stampede, thinking in a detached way that she'd picked the wrong day to be late for class.

A frightened crowd gathered outside the university's student center, pressing toward the doors and shouting over the siren. Careen fought to keep her balance in the undulating mob. The shrieking siren cut off abruptly, and in the unnerving silence, phones all around her pinged with incoming messages. She dug hers out of her back pocket.

"Campus alert. Shut up--it's a campus alert." The murmurs spread and seemed to calm the crowd. Hundreds of phones played the voice message in near-unison, magnifying the audio so it was easily heard:

"The Office of Civilian Safety and Defense confirmed that a chemical weapons attack against the United States is imminent. Terrorists have released a latent cocktail of poisons into the atmosphere, where it can remain, inert, until such time as they choose to detonate it. You are directed to report to a designated distribution center in your area to receive an antidote that will protect you. Weekly allotments of this antidote will be provided free of charge for as long as the threat persists. The OCSD expects the terrorists to mount repeated attacks, so it is essential that you take the recommended daily dosage. Compliance is a small price to pay for your safety."

Every face turned toward the cloudless, blue sky as someone's sobs cut through the silence.

9:47 AM

Careen fidgeted as she stood in the slow-moving queue. She'd been anxious to get inside the building and away from the danger that lurked overhead, but the informational video playing in the vestibule did nothing to quell her fears. According to the video, an attack could occur at any time; when it did, there would be no flash, no warning, no odor…and no place to hide. But taking the Counteractive System of Defense antidote would render the poison ineffectual. According to the video, the OCSD had the situation under control, and there was no reason to worry.

But Careen could think of plenty to worry about. For starters, she worried that, unlike her, most of the people in line seemed to dismiss the danger after they watched the video message. A group of girls behind her were chattering like they were at a party. She could hear people all around her telling each other not to worry, it's just another attack. It's no big deal. We hear about them all the time. *They wouldn't say that if they'd ever been in real danger. They honestly don't believe anything bad can happen to them.*

The workers distributed the antidote so slowly that Careen feared the attack would be long over before she made it through the line, and though she hoped she'd be done in time for her afternoon classes, she knew she had no choice but to wait. Denying the threat wouldn't help, and a 4.0 GPA wouldn't save her.

"Our protest might even get coverage on PeopleCam! My mom has a friend whose daughter knows a guy that works there. They're probably sending a crew over."

Careen looked around in amazement. "What are you protesting? Are you against taking the antidote?"

The girl wrinkled her nose. "No! We're protesting against *terrorism*. Terrorism should stop. Right. Now. So once we take our antidote we're going to stand outside and sing songs and show those terrorists that we're not afraid. Like the flower children in Vietnam a hundred years ago."

"Umm…wow. Some of the pertinent details aside, Vietnam was still a totally different situation." *Idiot.*

"We can make a difference if we ask all the terrorists to give peace and understanding a chance."

"Oh my gosh! I bet none of our leaders ever thought to try that. You ought to call the president." The girl looked smug, and Careen, already on edge, exploded. "Have you been living in some kind of reality-free zone? What do you know about protesting or terrorism—or anything, for that matter? You might as well be a herd of sheep."

The girl turned away and spoke loudly to her friends. "Did you hear what she just said? *She's* an authority on terrorism." Several people were staring in their direction, and one of the distribution workers patrolling the lines looked Careen up and down and noted something on her clipboard. Defiantly, Careen got out her own notebook and scribbled a few lines, mimicking the woman's actions. Soon the woman dropped her gaze and moved away, leaving only the buzz of quiet conversation to fill the void.

Careen tried to shut out the memories that replayed in her head, but she'd never forget the way shards of glass and other debris had rained down on the café table that sheltered her. How her ears rang from the blast and her eyes watered from the cloud of smoke and dust that lingered. Most of all she remembered the blinding flash of light and her father's hands on her back as he shoved her to the floor, hard. She hadn't seen that attack coming. She'd been a kid. Now that she was on her own, she had to take care of herself.

She was startled out of her unpleasant meditation by an exasperated voice nearby.

"But what's in it? Is it safe? Can you at least tell me if it's been tested?"

A young couple was at the front of the line. The man leaned toward the distribution worker, palms planted on the table. "My wife is pregnant. She's not taking *anything* unless we know it's safe for her and the baby. Let me talk to whoever's in charge here!"

The people around Careen began to shift and crane their necks to get a better view. She stood on tiptoe, hoping to hear the answer to his question, and watched with growing horror as a security officer grabbed the man and forced his arm back into a painful hold. His wife burst into tears as the guard shoved him through the crowd. He tried to twist free, but more guards surrounded them. Careen heard the thwack of a nightstick—once, twice, three times. Two guards dragged him toward the exit, while another took his sobbing wife by the arm and forced her to follow.

The door banged shut behind them, and the remaining guards returned to their positions along the wall. No one in line made a sound. Careen clutched her notebook to her chest and bowed her head.

9:59 AM

Tommy Bailey lay tangled in his blankets, one arm hanging off the side of the bed. He usually slept soundly, thanks to his pain meds, but not today. He opened his eyes, blinking back the bright sunshine that filled the room. *What the hell was that noise?* He glanced at his bedside clock. Only 10 AM? He'd have slept much later if not for that siren howling outside, but now that he was awake, he was curious enough to roll out of bed and hobble downstairs. The television in the living room was on, which was no surprise since it powered up automatically any time there was an important announcement or mandatory programming. He lowered himself onto the sofa to find out what was going on.

"OCSD expects repeated large-scale attacks. The National Weather Service, in cooperation with the OCSD, will monitor the atmosphere and report discernible toxin levels. The Emergency Broadcast System will conduct practice drills and notify the public in the event of an actual chemical attack. Remember, the antidote will counteract the effects of hazardous toxins if taken every day, so for the next three weeks, the Emergency Broadcast System will issue morning reminders to help everyone acclimate to the dosage schedule. Take action to protect yourself and your family. Your safety is our greatest concern. Go directly to the distribution center in your quadrant."

The OCSD's PeopleNet address and an information hotline number flashed on the screen.

Tommy shook the cobwebs from his head. *Do I want to live or die? Shit. Not again.*

10:48 AM

Tommy limped down the porch steps, crutches in hand. It was almost a mile to the nearest distribution center, and in his current state, traveling there and back on foot was going to take hours. He hadn't been that far from home on his own since before the accident.

Just then the mailman came up the walk with a pile of catalogs. Tommy knew without looking that they'd be addressed to Lara Bailey. The mailman glanced at him uncomfortably, and stepped around him to put the mail in the box.

"Thanks."

"Sure. You doing okay?"

"Yeah." Tommy busied himself with his crutches.

"If you wanna stop getting all them catalogs, you just gotta message the companies, ya know?"

"Yeah. I'll get around to it."

The mailman nodded and continued on his way.

Tommy swung onto his crutches and headed toward the university campus, a little surprised that he wanted to live badly enough to go get the antidote. *I guess I still have some fight left in me, even after everything that's happened in the last four months.*

After the accident, he'd spent two weeks in the hospital, most of it a hazy memory distorted by pain and whatever it was that dripped numbingly into his veins from an IV line. Four surgeries later, the shattered bones in his right leg were held together with metal plates and screws. His visible scars were healing, but the doctors offered no guarantees that he'd ever walk normally, let alone make a full recovery. To Tommy, a full recovery seemed impossible.

He'd turned eighteen while he was in the hospital.

He hadn't been able to attend his parents' funeral.

He wasn't sure how to live without everything he'd lost, but he guessed he hadn't given up. Not yet.

12:02 PM

Careen sighed with relief when she reached the head of the line, put her notes away, and fished out her ID. The middle-aged woman at the folding table peered through her reading glasses, found Careen's name on the distribution list, then weighed her and took a DNA swab. The employee with the clipboard approached the table and bent close to whisper something in her ear. The woman who was helping Careen studied her through narrowed eyes for a moment, seemed to reach a conclusion about her, and applied a red sticker next to her name on the list. Then she held out a small, white, cardboard box.

"What does that mean?"

"What, dear?"

"The sticker next to my name. What does it mean?" She pointed at the list. There was only one other red sticker on the page.

"Oh, nothing. Just a discretionary dot, is all."

"A discretionary *what*? Whose discretion?"

"Mine." The woman pushed the box into her hand then looked to the girl in line behind her. "Next!"

Careen clutched the box and glanced around as she stepped away from the table. Most people were taking their doses immediately. Some of the girls were crying. *Can this stuff really keep me safe?* She tore open the box, pulled out her bottle, and quickly read the label. 'Three drops daily. Mild side effects may include headache, dizziness, unusually vivid dreams…' *Great, whatever. It doesn't really matter. I have to protect myself.*

Careen dropped the bottle in her bag as she strolled past the guards, the tiny orange drops leaving a bitter taste on her tongue.

As she crossed the lobby, she noticed a guy on crutches struggling to squeeze his way through the heavy doors. In her hurry to help, Careen's leg became entangled with the young man's crutches, creating a near-catastrophic pile-up.

He shook his blond hair out of his eyes and focused on righting himself, his narrow, angry gaze fixed somewhere over her head as she steadied him.

"Oh my gosh, I'm so sorry." Her brain felt fuzzy, and she was lightheaded all of a sudden. *Am I slurring my words? So embarrassing.*

"Don't worry about it." He shifted his weight and took a step.

"No, I mean it. Just trying to help." Even though he was obviously trying to get away from her, she kept her hand pressed to his chest as her own pulse thudded in her ears. *What is going on?*

"Look, can you maybe get out of my way?"

"Umm, yeah. Sure." She swayed in his wake as she let him pass, and when he was out of sight, she walked out of the student center into a blinding pink light. She could see herself in full color, unaffected, and as everything else receded into a pink fog, a sense of calm and well-being washed over her. The light warmed her face, and she breathed in the sweet smell of cotton candy.

She wandered across campus, smiling blithely. At first she felt alone, as if she were in a spotlight, but soon she noticed other people out walking, too, and it was fun to watch them grow closer and materialize out of the bright cherry haze. Her messenger bag was getting heavy, so she took out one of her thick notebooks and tossed it in a trash bin. That was when she recognized a guy who was in one of her classes; and as she noticed his broad shoulders and how his dark hair curled out from under the edges of his baseball cap, it was like she was really seeing him for the first time. She stared at him, acutely aware of the nerve endings in her spine, sure that the tingling rush of energy spreading through her body had to be coming from him. She boldly caught his eye.

He walked straight up to her, grabbed a handful of hair at the base of her neck, tilted back her head, and kissed her. When the kiss ended he smiled, and she followed him into the fog.

2:28 PM

The distribution center's line was long and inched forward almost imperceptibly. Tommy wished he'd brought something to eat. He felt faint from exerting himself on the long walk, and was pretty sure he'd collapse to the floor without his crutches to hold him up. Someone jostled him from behind, and he turned around, irritated.

"Sorry, dude. Oh...hey, Tommy." It was one of his teammates from high school. The boy extended his hand uncomfortably, and when Tommy didn't respond, he settled for a halfhearted fake punch on Tommy's shoulder.

"Hey."

"I heard about...what happened. Sorry about your folks. I mean, I meant to stop by, you know; a bunch of us were going to come see how you were doing but things got so busy...what with starting university and all. Umm…so how you been? I mean…oh God, sorry. That was stupid." He avoided Tommy's eyes.

"I'm great. You?"

"Yeah, really great, except for this whole thing today. Everyone's freaked out, you know? They even canceled the party at my frat house tonight. Some crazy shit, huh?"

"Yeah. Some crazy shit."

"Well, take care of yourself, right? See you around?"

"Sure."

4:16 PM

Tommy tottered through the front door, using a crutch to slam it shut behind him. He was sweating from head to toe, and his recently healed incision hurt so much he feared it had pulled apart somewhere along the fifteen-inch scar. It was definitely past time for a pain pill. Too bad there wasn't a pill to help him be around other people without feeling conspicuous and defective. *Why is it that every interaction I have with anyone focuses on my shortcomings? I couldn't even open the stupid door by myself.*

He knew it was partly his fault that he was alone. Art and Beth Severson, his parents' best friends, had encouraged him to stay with them after he was discharged from the hospital, and he'd taken them up on the offer for a couple weeks. They'd infiltrated his drug-induced fog with good intentions and regular mealtimes. Beth hovered over him with a cheery efficiency that he found annoying, and Art asked so many questions about the accident that Tommy had finally gotten tired of saying "I don't remember" and clammed up. Every evening Art watched the SportsCam channel on TV, which only served to remind Tommy, the former athlete, of his new physical limitations. Maybe Art had felt obligated to be there for his dead best friend's son, but Tommy wished he didn't. He'd found the whole situation intolerable, and as soon as he was able to get around on his own, he'd gone home.

He pulled the little white box from the pocket of his hoodie and removed the amber bottle inside. Three drops daily. Not just for him…for everyone. Everyone was in danger; everyone was scared. He wasn't alone in this fight.

He limped into the kitchen for a glass of water and a pain pill. With three tiny drops of the antidote swirling in his glass, he washed down the pill with a single gulp. Back in the living room, he flopped on the sofa and closed his eyes, and soon the sofa was breathing softly, and he was somewhere else, his body rising and falling in time with the sofa, like waves on the lake he'd frequented with his parents. He was afloat on sunlit water, the bright light sparkling and changing in kaleidoscopic patterns as he drifted aimlessly. In the distance, a pretty brunette walked alone on the shore.

5:12 PM
Quadrant BG-098 (formerly Knox County, Kentucky)

Wes Carraway flipped over the sign on the diner's window to CLOSED, locked the front door, and drew the blinds. He crossed the room and slapped the counter to get his older brother's attention. Mitch came out of the kitchen, wiping his hands on his apron, and pulled a little amber bottle out of his pocket.

"This is the one, Wes. The one he warned me about. This chemical-weapons attack is all over the news! Of course there's nothing to report so they're all saying stuff like "up next, a live report from so-and-so at blah-blah-blah." But if you ask me, the whole thing feels staged."

"Just so you know, you sound like the true disciple of a conspiracy theorist."

"Yeah? Well, if this is such a huge threat, why are the alleged terrorists holding off until we've all had time to take the antidote? Whatever happened to a good old-fashioned sneak attack? Shoot, that's what I'd do."

"You'd make a great terrorist."

"Hell, I'd make a great world leader, 'cause I understand peer pressure and threats. If you tell people they're being attacked, they'll stand in line for hours to let you take away their freedoms. All you need is a rallying point like—"

"How about, 'it's a small price to pay for your safety'?"

"Or something like that. Nice observation, Mr. Quadrant Marshal."

"Ha, ha." *Like I'd dare say anything else in his presence.* "So since I came all the way out here to see you, how about you make me some pancakes before I go? I'm starting a new assignment tomorrow: babysitting the little darlings over in the university quadrant. OP-439."

"Yeah? Going uptown, huh? Well, babysit all you like. You're no older than they are, so have some fun with a debutante or two, but don't forget why you're really there. Get us back in the loop so we can get to work."

Wes spun the antidote bottle on the countertop. It stopped with the cap pointing between them. "You figure we're safe when we take this stuff?"

Mitch laughed. "I figure I'm safer when I *don't* take it."

"You're not going to?"

"Aw, come on, little brother. We're so far behind the times in this corner of West By-God that if the world ends tomorrow, we won't even hear about it for a couple years."

"What if they come in after you?"

"They who? The OCSD or the terrorists? Either way, let 'em try. I can hide out back in the hills if I need to."

Wes rolled his eyes but grinned in spite of himself. "Yeah, I know you can. So how about those pancakes?"

Chapter 2

The United States had slumped into a prolonged recession during the first three decades of the twenty-first century, and different terrorist groups took advantage of the nation's preoccupation with its economic woes, relentlessly attacking stadiums, shopping malls, airports, and high-rise office buildings. In desperation, the president ordered the creation of the Office of Civilian Safety and Defense in 2019. The OCSD immediately implemented a quadrant marshal system to increase security, and the nation was re-platted into a grid of two-square mile quadrants, with marshals assigned to do everything possible to safeguard homes and citizens from small, localized attacks. Often this included monitoring the activities of the people they were there to protect. But it was a small price to pay for everyone's safety.

Everyone was strongly encouraged to work at home and shop online, and soon most shopping malls and office buildings stood vacant. When the OCSD restricted air travel for pleasure, people accessed the larger world solely by watching the government-controlled PeopleCam, SportsCam, and VacationCam networks on television.

The changes seemed to work for a while, so when the attacks began again, the OCSD countered with more safety-enhancing Civilian Restrictions.

In 2021, the OCSD foiled a plot to blow up bridges in ten different cities simultaneously. Because the bombs were made of ordinary items purchased at hardware stores, the OCSD recommended that cash be abolished and all purchases be made with government-issued debit cards so the OCSD would be able to monitor and track anyone who bought items that could be made into something dangerous.

A deadly airborne virus, released at one hundred supermarkets in 2024, prompted the OCSD to recommend the creation of the Essential Services Department to make weekly home food deliveries so no one would have to risk his or her life shopping for groceries. Though the plan faced some opposition from the public, Congress passed the necessary laws without hesitation, and all grocery stores became off-limits to the public. The Essential Services Department's nutritionists planned menus and determined how much each family needed to eat. Logistical engineers organized a weekly delivery schedule, and the Payables Department automatically deducted the cost of food from everyone's government-issued debit accounts. The program turned out to be more costly than anticipated, and those who couldn't afford to spend additional money on food ate only what was delivered to their homes. Before long, a great many restaurants were out of business.

A rash of car bombings in 2027 led the OCSD to outlaw personal vehicles, except for government employees and a select group of wealthy and powerful civilians in the private sector. It was too risky to allow ordinary citizens access to such large potential weapons. Just two years before, the OCSD decreed that, since large public gatherings attracted terrorist activity, concerts and sporting events should be closed to live audiences.

But even with all the safety measures in place, random attacks were still commonplace, especially in the urban quadrants. Stress and worry eroded the people's will, and they lived in constant fear. Parents forgot to teach their children to be brave.

In October 2034, OCSD director Dr. Lowell Stratford advised the president and Congress of a plot to use chemical weapons in a widespread attack against the entire nation. Stratford promised the president that the OCSD's elite team of scientists wouldn't rest until they'd developed an antidote—and they would do it before the terrorists could put the finishing touches on their deadly chemical weapon cocktail.

8:02 AM
Distribution Day minus 10: October 17, 2034
Office of Civilian Safety and Defense
Quadrant DC-001 (formerly Washington, DC)

Dr. Trina Jacobs pressed her thumb to the scanner on the wall and waited for an affirmative beep. The door to her lab slid open, and she stepped inside.

"Save us, Dr. Jacobs!" A jumble of voices cried out to her—men, women, and children. "Help us! Please…"

Trina gritted her teeth and kept moving across the room. She heard those plaintive cries every time she stepped into her lab, because the director believed the recorded message would motivate her to complete her task at top speed. She'd been on the job for almost a month, and the sound of those voices still made her feel sick to her stomach.

She signed on to her computer and retrieved the results from yesterday's tests. Her most recent attempt at an antidote had been too strong—it blocked the effects of all the known poisons, but killed human cells in the process. Another failure.

"It can't be done. He's asking the impossible," she muttered. "No wonder they gave up trying to cure the common cold. Too many variables."

"Your attitude is unacceptable, Dr. Jacobs. Everyone in this country is counting on you." Dr. Lowell Stratford's face appeared on her computer screen. The director was always listening in. Butting in. *I gotta stop talking to myself.*

"Sir, you know as well as I do…"

"I know it's time we protect the American public. We're moving on to the next phase of the project. Quite a waste of taxpayer dollars hiring an expensive team of researchers and doctors, since I was the one who found the solution to the problem."

A document file replaced Dr. Stratford's face on the screen. Trina clicked on the file to open it.

TOP SECRET
From: Lowell Stratford, Ph.D.
Date: October 17, 2034
Re: Distribution of prophylactic Counteractive System of Defense (CSD), Phase One

On Friday, October 27, 2034, the American public will be notified of an imminent chemical weapons attack against our country. We expect the announcement to cause widespread concern, even panic; in response, a telephone hotline and PeopleNet site have been created to address FAQ. Information concerning the attack will be broadcast on PeopleCam, all corner news tickers, and subscription news services. The automated communication centers will likely be inadequate to handle the influx of inquiries, so they will simply deliver a recorded message advising the caller to remain calm.

We expect the public's concern and panic to subside once they take the first dose of CSD. Hotline calls and visits to the PeopleNet site should dwindle rapidly to a manageable level.

This three-phase plan is expected to help our citizens cope with the daily threat of terrorism in Phase One, stabilize the floundering economy in Phase Two, and prepare an estimated eighty percent of the adult population for participation in Phase Three.

"What the..." Trina grabbed her phone and dialed the main lab. "Kevin? Bring me a sample of what Stratford's been working on."

10:30 AM

Trina Jacobs jumped to her feet, slamming both palms against the conference room table. "You're calling it a Counteractive System of Defense? Really? How about just calling it lysergic acid diethylamide?"

Dr. Lowell Stratford rolled his eyes impatiently. "Well of course we can't call it *that*!"

"But it's nothing more than LSD mixed with scopolamine," Trina cried. "That's not an antidote! We have no right to do this to the American people—or to anyone, for that matter! They're not lab rats, for God's sake!"

"Oh, but we do. Congress granted the Office of Civilian Safety and Defense the authority to implement any antiterrorism programs we deem necessary, and this definitely qualifies as such. The constant threat of terrorism has destroyed the psyche of the average American. The economy is in shambles. No one's buying or selling anything because they think we're going to get blown to hell at any moment. The health care system is crashing because we can't tax the people fast enough to cover the cost of their free psychological care. We need an equalizer, and we need it fast!"

Trina surveyed the room, but none of the other scientists would make eye contact with her. "Are any of you listening to this? No one here thinks we have a problem?" She glared at Dr. Stratford. "Okay. I get it. Everyone in this room participated in your clinical trial, right? You've medicated and brainwashed your alleged team of experts?"

"Of course not," Stratford said, sneering. "No one on the team is permitted to take CSD. We have to remain clear-headed to implement the entire plan. And don't forget, Dr. Jacobs, we have every right under the law to pacify the American public with hallucinogenic drugs, but we're not required to *tell* them what they're taking! Call it soda. Call it cough syrup. Call it anything but LSD! I think this discussion is over. We're ready to begin Phase One."

He pushed the red button on his touch screen and two burly security officers entered the conference room.

Trina hung her head. The rest of the team applauded. The security guards escorted Trina to a windowless room down the hall and locked her inside.

Stupid stupid stupid. Think before you speak. Her eyes darted about the room, focusing at last on the darkened television screen mounted to the adjacent wall. She addressed the screen, hands on hips. "I know you can hear me, Stratford. I'm not going to be one of your lab rats."

Trina whirled around as the door crashed open. Dr. Stratford entered, flanked by his guards. "Actually, you are. You're getting the very first dose of CSD. How about a week's worth, lab rat? What do you think that'll do to you?"

The guards pinned Trina against the wall, holding her arms at her sides. She turned her head away and kicked at Dr. Stratford. He dodged her impatiently as the guards redoubled their efforts to subdue her. Stratford stepped closer, forced her mouth open, and squeezed in a full syringe of an orange liquid. Within seconds, Trina stopped fighting.

11:15 AM

The clatter of Madalyn Davies's heels echoed off the marble floor as she followed Dr. Stratford down the hall. She didn't miss a step; her perfectly manicured nails kept perfect time on her tablet.

"All essential personnel should be issued the alternate formula of CSD. We'll need to flag their profiles in the main database to minimize any mix-ups. Nationwide distribution starts in a week."

"Who's classified as essential, sir?"

"Post office. IRS. Food Distribution. Quadrant Marshals. Everyone who works at the factories that manufacture CSD. And the employees at the distribution centers."

"And they won't realize they're taking a placebo?"

"Shouldn't. They may experience some of the listed side effects, most of which will be purely psychosomatic. Most importantly, they'll remain clear-headed and able to carry out daily tasks without experiencing anxiety. It's the non-essential workers who may find the side effects more...debilitating. They'll be markedly distracted. Less concerned with what's going on around them."

"But once Phase One is underway, how will we monitor everyone? How can we make sure they're doing what they're supposed to?"

Stratford stopped, turned toward her, and leaned closer. Madalyn, encouraged by the familiarity, tossed her long blonde hair over her shoulder and tilted her head so it was almost touching his as he spoke. "We borrowed a few tricks from the military for this one—each time a citizen opens their bottle, a microchip in the cap sends a radio-frequency message to OCSD's main computer. We can keep tabs on who has "checked in," so to speak. That way we can send the quadrant marshals out to remind anyone who forgets. Our citizens need to develop good habits, because cooperation is key in Phase Two. Then, once they are used to thinking more collectively, it will naturally pave the way for Phase Three, which requires a larger commitment and more active participation if our country is going to win the war on terrorism once and for all."

"Oh, and sir, how about the press—which formula do they get?"

Stratford snorted. "Like anyone could tell the difference with that bunch of idiots."

Chapter 3

8:58 AM
Day 2: Saturday, October 28, 2034
Quadrant OP-439

Careen woke in the semidarkness and saw Christmas lights dangling haphazardly from a window frame. *But it isn't Christmas.* The lights weren't lit. She was definitely someplace she'd never been before.

She was lying on her side, and able to glance around without lifting her head. The room was messy, and the sheets had an unfamiliar smell. She spied her bag hanging from the back of a chair. As she became more aware of her surroundings, she realized that she wasn't wearing any clothes. Her confusion turned to panic when she felt someone stir beside her. *Oh Jeez.* She held her breath and squeezed her eyes shut, hoping this was some kind of crazy dream.

She jumped at the disaster siren's three sharp blasts and ruined her chances of slipping away unnoticed. She looked guiltily over her shoulder. A boy with dark curly hair lay face down on his pillow. *Oh crap oh crap oh crap. Who is that? Where am I?*

"Take your dose immediately." A woman's voice came over the loudspeakers.

Careen leaped out of bed, pulled on a random t-shirt she picked up off the floor, and scrabbled through her bag for the little bottle.

He was awake. Out of the corner of her eye, she saw his biceps tighten as he slid to the edge of the bed and reached for his own bottle on the nightstand.

Careen placed three drops of the orange liquid on her tongue and tossed the bottle back into her bag. She spotted her jeans and sweater lying on the floor nearby and reached for them, and then paused because shiny pink bubbles were dancing from her fingertips. She held her hands out in front of her and watched the bubbles grow larger. Intrigued, she forgot she was in a hurry and flicked her fingers to send the bubbles floating into the air. More bubbles sprouted, faster and larger, and she wiggled her fingers so the stream spiraled and twisted, filling the space around her. She heard the bed squeak as he rolled over, and she turned to face him.

He lay back against the pillows, smiling at her through the bubbly haze like she was something amazing, something unexpected. Her face grew hot, but not from embarrassment. She took a deep breath and realized she didn't need the t-shirt after all.

9:07 AM

Tommy put away the little bottle, shut the medicine cabinet, and peered out the bathroom window. The sun wasn't coming out and he wasn't fixing his hair. There was no point, since he wasn't going anywhere. Besides, he looked better with bed head. He scrubbed both hands through his hair to prove his point.

The sky wasn't blue, or black, or white. It was just...off. A rumble of thunder echoed in the distance as he stumbled downstairs to the kitchen. There was cereal, but then again, there was always cereal. Milk was not guaranteed, but today there were a few drops left in the carton. He yawned and flopped on the couch with a bowl of Cookie Crisp. With milk.

He turned on the television and found an old movie to watch while he ate. He'd seen it several times, but this time the awkward tilt of his head skewed the picture. A bunch of hoodlums were shooting it out with the police in an alley. His cereal tasted more like cardboard than cookies. As he watched, grass began to sprout in the movie-set alley. It grew so fast it obscured a dumpster and the fire escape, and no one knew where to aim their guns. *Hmm... I don't remember that ever happening before.*

A message from the Emergency Broadcast System flashed across the bottom of the screen: REMINDING YOU TO TAKE YOUR DAILY DOSE OF CSD. IT'S A SMALL PRICE TO PAY FOR YOUR SAFETY. Tommy saluted with his spoon.

Thunder crashed, but sunlight flooded the room. He shifted his gaze to watch raindrops run down the wall and puddle on the floor.

The dense grass spread from the television into the living room, which was impossible, but somehow Tommy didn't care. He wiggled his toes inside his dad's old pair of woolen slippers on his feet. His left foot cooperated, but the toes on his right foot barely moved. Even though he was used to it, he fought down a twinge of panic. He looked down at his right leg. Yesterday the fifteen-inch-long scar had pulsed red and purple. Today he couldn't see it at all. But it was there. It was definitely there.

The doorbell rang, and Tommy limped to the front door and stepped out onto the porch, but no one was there. Sunshine-ringed puddles lined the street. It was too early for the mail.

The leaves on the tree in his front yard were shockingly green for this late in the season. He heard another rumble—much closer and definitely not thunder. Five football players in full gear rushed the porch, knocking him back through the screen door and onto the floor. From the bottom of the pile, Tommy gasped for breath. A giant blade of grass brushed the ceiling.

9:57 AM

Wes Carraway stretched the kinks from his back as he crossed the parking lot. That quick trip home had made for a hell of a long commute to his new post in OP-439, but Wes knew better than to ignore a summons from his brother.

Mitch had raised Wes to be just like him—a government-hating, conspiracy-seeking nut. It had been Mitch's idea for Wes to enroll in quadrant marshal cadet school, and though Wes lacked his brother's anti-government fervor, he'd still been the most jaded and, in his mind, well-educated cadet in the program. He'd realized early on that it was best to keep his opinions and his family to himself if he wanted a career in the marshals; now, after three years on the job, no one at work even suspected he had a brother. Wes wasn't about to mention him; if he did, they'd both be arrested for treason.

Mitch was hell-bent on building a network of rebels like himself, and every so often he'd ask Wes to search the QM's criminal records database for someone or other. Mitch wanted no personal acquaintances in his network, to make it harder to identify other Resistance members through business or social contacts. Mitch insisted on using secret codes and fake names, and as a result, the members of the Resistance were like random pieces from different jigsaw puzzles—even when you examined them carefully, they didn't connect.

Last summer one of Mitch's contacts had been on the verge of going public with evidence of some sort of conspiracy, but died in a mysterious car crash before he had the chance. Mitch was obsessed with discovering the missing information, and demanded Wes help him. He gave him a name. Not a code name. A *real* name.

Wes had begged off at first. Too risky. He could lose his job. Go to jail. But now for the first time, he was willing to take any risk to get some answers. He knew something Mitch didn't know, and it was bugging the hell out of him. He paced the parking lot, afraid someone might sense his rage if he even thought about it inside a government building.

At his old quadrant marshal station, they'd made the entire staff take the antidote first thing in the morning, before the public even knew about the danger. Thanks to Mitch, Wes was naturally suspicious of anything that had to do with the OCSD, but he couldn't very well refuse the drug in the presence of all his coworkers. He took the dose but quit worrying about it when he didn't experience any side effects. He'd been afraid that Mitch would stick to his principles and end up getting sick from the poison, so he'd slipped a dose into his coffee to prove to him that it was safe. Within minutes Mitch had started acting really strange and mellow—he'd even stopped talking, for Pete's sake. That is, until Wes asked him about the Resistance. Then he told Wes stuff he'd never, ever have revealed, even if tortured for it.

"In the years since the Restrictions went into effect, I've helped members of the Resistance infiltrate government offices, especially in intelligence and security. There are a few members of Congress willing to feed me information, but you can't always count on those guys to be loyal. There's a hotshot kid, a video game designer, who's also into real-life explosives. They all hate Stratford and the OCSD. They're biding their time, waiting for a call to action. Don't count us out. Don't think we won't win in the end." He didn't seem to know or care what he was saying.

Wes had stayed with his brother much later than he'd intended. After about ten hours, the effects of the dose seemed to be waning, so he'd hit the road and left Mitch to sleep it off. He'd taken that antidote bottle with him, and then spent most of the six-hour drive trying to forget what his brother had told him. That was need-to-know stuff. And he *definitely* didn't need to know.

Now, bleary-eyed and stiff from the long drive, he walked into the unfamiliar lobby and reported to the duty officer, who directed him down the hall to an office outfitted with several computer ports. He slid into a seat and introduced himself to the marshal seated nearby. "Hey. Wes Carraway. Just got assigned here as an investigator."

"Henry Nelson." They shook hands.

"What're we doing?"

"Troublemakers."

Carraway grinned. "At cadet school they tried to train that out of me. Not that they succeeded."

Nelson sat up straighter. "Actually, we're assessing residents of this quadrant who were identified as potential troublemakers on Distribution Day." He gestured toward the computer in front of him. Carraway signed on.

Ironic. I'm digging into the lives of students in an attempt to find dissidents. Bet the QMs would crap themselves if they could get their hands on my brother. And me.

He opened the first file. Brainy kid from the wrong side of the tracks with excellent standardized test scores and grades. Victory Scholarship recipient. Two days ago, she'd been observed "creating a disturbance" and "making contact with a suspected terrorist." He rolled his eyes. Her roommate probably informed on her because she borrowed a sweater without asking or something.

But the suspected terrorist's name was all too familiar. *Wow. If I'd known he lived in OP-439 I'd have requested a transfer long ago.*

He clicked on the video link and watched surveillance footage of a dark-haired young woman. Her interaction with the suspected terrorist would look perfectly benign to the untrained eye.

But was she trying to join the Resistance or infiltrate it? He paused the video and took a good, long look at her. Either way, she could lead him to what he needed. He downloaded the file to his phone and glanced over his shoulder before he classified the file "no additional surveillance necessary." He wanted this investigation all to himself.

Chapter 4

7:28 AM
Day 4: Monday, October 30, 2034
Quadrant NY-917 (formerly mid-town Manhattan)

A pretty young reporter for PeopleCam's early-morning show posed with a street view behind her, smoothed her coat collar and waited for her cue. Her producer, standing beside the camera, had been listening intently into his earpiece. Now he snapped his fingers to get her attention.

"Hang on. We gotta scrap your story. We're going live with breaking news. They're going to feed it to me over my tablet. This could be the moment that makes your career, honey. Just read what it says. And...go!" He held his tablet under the camera lens where the reporter could see it.

"This just in from the Office of Civilian Safety and Defense. Life-threatening levels of chemical weapons are now present in the atmosphere over sections of the country, which means the terrorists have made good on their threat. Though this is *not* a drill, the OCSD stresses that if you live in an affected area and you've been taking your CSD as instructed, it's perfectly safe to go about your daily business."

The disaster alert sirens began to wail in the background. The reporter glanced over her shoulder and saw people scrambling and pushing their way into any shelter they could find. The producer motioned for her to keep reading.

"I repeat—this is not a drill, but there is no reason for concern. We must have faith that we are safe. We are protected by the efforts of our government. Rest assured that we will be...just...well, just fine."

As soon as the producer indicated they were clear, the reporter covered her mouth and nose with her hands and ran for cover.

She staggered in her high heels as she dodged a heavyset, bald man with a tattoo of the sun covering the right half of his face. The man shouted after her. "The end is near! Woo-hoooo!"

In the middle of the intersection, he threw open his arms, leaned back and took a deep breath. "Come on, bring it! I got nothing else to do today! Hit me with your best shot!" He pumped his fist at the sky and, still shouting, ran past the camera. The PeopleCam producer panned to follow him down the deserted street until he turned a corner and disappeared from sight.

9:00 AM
Quadrant OP-439

Eduardo Rodriguez was late for work. He should have been out delivering the mail, but he didn't like to leave his apartment until he made sure it was safe, so he sat on his tattered sofa and surfed the television channels for news of discernible toxin levels. On PeopleCam, the word *martyr* was superimposed in large red letters over a still photo of a tattooed man, and Eduardo's stomach lurched in fear. PeopleCam's news anchors Pete Sheridan and Sheila Roth looked grim and determined as Pete read the top story.

"About an hour ago, a fear-crazed man became the first casualty of today's terror attack. Sid Friedman, a resident of NY-917, succumbed to the toxins in the air soon after this video was recorded by a PeopleCam news crew. Witnesses on the scene reported Friedman was yelling incoherently and pointing at the sky."

The screen showed silent footage of Sid Friedman running down the street, arms flailing wildly about. Eduardo grimaced. It looked like the poison must hurt. "Preliminary reports suggest Friedman failed to take an adequate dose of CSD and was unable to survive today's chemical attack."

Sheila tilted her head, waited a beat, then turned to address her co-anchor. "That's a lesson for us all, Pete."

"I agree. Are you taking your CSD, Sheila?"

"You better believe it, Pete. I'm not taking any chances."

"Well, that's good to know because we certainly can't get along without you! So Sheila, what's your favorite way to take CSD? I think our viewers at home might like to know." Pete winked conspiratorially and patted Sheila's hand. "It takes a little getting used to, don't you think? Kind of bitter—I don't mind it straight up, but it's even better when you put it in a Bloody Mary!"

Sheila aimed a dazzling smile at the camera and let Pete laugh at his own witty remark as she resumed the day's top story. "Friedman, who had no family, will be buried with honors in the national cemetery." She shook her head. "Such a tragic loss of life."

Eduardo turned off the newscast. Even though there weren't any dangerous levels of toxins reported in his quadrant right now, an attack could happen while he was out. He broke into a sweat just thinking about it. *Soldiers have to be brave.* He went into the kitchen and poured himself a couple fingers of Kahlúa, then added three drops from his bottle of CSD and swirled it around, watching the orange blend into the milky brown.

Just while I'm working. He gulped it down noisily, wiped his mustache with the back of his hand, grabbed his keys, and went forth into battle.

9:09 AM
Day 6: Wednesday, November 1, 2034
Quadrant DC-001

Trina was vaguely aware of being carried, the way her grandpa had carried her when she was little. When she was older, they'd often walked hand-in-hand to the corner market. "We'd better get us some peaches. Can't have a visit from my best girl without we get us some peaches." He'd stepped along briskly, smiling down at her. His stride was short, with just the hint of an old man's shuffle.

Trina let go of her grandfather's hand and stepped away from him. He smiled encouragingly, nodding. He seemed to understand that people were in trouble and she needed to save them. She prayed that God would help her know what to do, and like magic she was sitting in the family's pew in a small country church with her mama and grandmother. Grandma smelled of talcum powder and waved a paper fan in the summer heat, just as ten generations of faithful ladies in that congregation had done. Trina, elbows on the back of the pew in front of her, closed her eyes and pressed her steepled fingers into her forehead.

"Save us, Dr. Jacobs!" cried the voices.

Do they mean my daddy? He's the doctor in town. I'm just a kid. I don't know how to save anybody.

Trina, now fourteen years old, sat across from her mother at the kitchen table. Breakfast was over, but the aromas of bacon and coffee still lingered. Her mama surveyed her sternly. "Child, you can grow up to be anything you want to be. But I won't let you be a liar, covering up for your no-account friend. I know it was her that stole that blouse. You can't fix other people's wrongs. You can't save her by taking the blame, you hear? I'll wear her out when I get hold of her. From now on, you take care of you.

"You're going places, Trina. You're smart. Gonna go to college and do big things. Don't let her sorry self get in the way of your life."

"Yes ma'am." Trina spoke through parched lips. She opened her eyes, blinking in the dim light, and tried to move her arms and legs, but they felt as if they didn't belong to her. *Where am I? In the hospital? I guess I've been sick. I can't remember. What's wrong with me?*

She sat up slowly, testing her mobility, and looked around for a call button. The door opened, and a lab assistant carrying an amber bottle entered the room. Before Trina could utter a word, he squeezed three drops of CSD into her mouth, and then helped her to her feet. She leaned on him heavily as he guided her down the hall and into a windowless room. The floor tiles shifted and spun beneath her feet as she walked, forcing her to step carefully.

"Here, Dr. Jacobs. Time to go to work." He seated her at the desk, flicked on the computer screen, and put her hand over the mouse. "Just click, okay?"

The screen flashed: CLICK NOW. Trina did.

2:26 PM

Lowell Stratford settled into his office chair to watch the rough cut of the "live" coverage of Sid Friedman's funeral. Tomorrow morning the funeral, which was, in his opinion, a masterpiece of pageantry and spectacle, would preempt all scheduled programming and interrupt any other communication in progress on phones, radios, televisions, and outdoor billboards so no one would accidentally forget to watch.

Stratford couldn't help but chuckle. *People say there's no convenient time for death or taxes, but Friedman's timing was perfect.* The OCSD's public relations team had handled all the details of the ceremony, and the in-house visual communications department had been working furiously, producing two new videos to be aired after the funeral coverage. The first video, *The Martyr and His Legacy*, portrayed Friedman as a patriot who sacrificed himself to test the limits of safety.

His failure to survive the first chemical attack served as a warning to the rest of the American people.

The second, entitled *Together, We Are Invincible*, began with soothing music and shots of happy people and beautiful scenes from nature, followed by images of peaceful villages, farms, and bustling cities. The narrator spoke over the images. "In past times of prosperity, some people believed they didn't need the level of guidance and protection from government that we enjoy today. This kind of thinking, unchecked, led to disorganization, recession, famine, and war. It made our country weak, and it made us easy prey for all sorts of disasters."

Stratford mouthed the words along with the narrator, which was easy since he'd written the script himself.

The music swelled. Different voices chimed in: "I don't need to wear a seat belt in the car."

"I can eat and drink as much as I want."

"I will grow whatever crops I choose."

"I can build my house on the edge of a cliff."

"I will decide what my children should and should not learn."

The images on the screen changed from comforting scenes of the contented to a staccato, rapidly edited sequence of car accidents, obese people, withered crops, sickness, collapsing buildings, homeless children, closed factories, soldiers in combat, and the final image: a skull and crossbones on black background.

"Ordinary people, left to their own devices, will not be prepared when disaster strikes. We must look to our leaders for protection from the dangers around us." The video concluded with the now-famous footage of Sid Friedman running down the street. The narrator had one last gem to share: "CSD is not a choice. It's the only way."

Stratford nodded with satisfaction. He made a note to have the OCSD's public relations department order more Sid Friedman posters.

Chapter 5

6:53 AM
Day 7: Thursday, November 2, 2034
Quadrant OP-439

Tommy heard nothing but the steady rhythm of his feet as he ran around the high school track. His breathing was ragged, but he was smiling as he backpedaled to a stop. He sagged against the chain-link fence, draped his arms across the top, and shook the sweat out of his hair, reveling in his pure exhaustion. The breeze smelled like fresh-cut grass.

When he opened his eyes and realized he'd been dreaming, his jubilation disappeared. He rolled over, and pain shot up his leg.

At exactly 9 AM, Tommy pulled his pillow over his head to muffle the bleating disaster siren and the female voice that reminded everyone to take their daily doses. *I don't feel like doing a damn thing when I take that stuff. I know, I know; some guy died when he didn't take his dose. But maybe, just this once, a few minutes won't make any difference.*

He dressed in shorts, a sweatshirt, and high socks to hide his scar, laced his running shoes, and limped defiantly past the amber bottle on his way out the door.

When he returned home forty-five minutes later, Tommy felt triumphant—not the way he had in his dream, but more like he'd gotten away with some misdeed. He'd managed an uneven trot for almost half a mile without falling. He'd stayed focused and persevered, despite the discomfort. He felt so good, he was already planning to sneak in another early-morning workout before the siren tomorrow.

With effort, he climbed the stairs to the bathroom, anxious for a shower. He slumped against the cool tile as the steamy water relaxed his muscles.

Three drops later, dewy grass crept across the bathroom floor and tickled his left foot as he brushed his teeth. He tried to ignore it, then to kick it away, but the grass was insistent. It wrapped itself around his good leg and yanked it out from under him, and he fell, hard.

When he regained consciousness, Tommy peered through the mist and realized he was in the wreckage of his parents' car. He could hear his dad saying "Get up. Get up, they're coming," but he couldn't move because the grass was holding him down. He closed his eyes and heard the rush of people approaching. A flashlight beam cut a yellow slash through the darkness behind his eyelids. His mom called out for him, but he was powerless. Rough hands gripped his shoulders. He couldn't save himself. *I can't save anyone.*

Tommy curled his knees toward his chest and covered his head as the wail of sirens echoed in his ears. The female voice on the loudspeaker crooned, "You'll never be what you should have been."

9:08 AM

Why is it so hard to keep track of that antidote bottle? Careen rummaged frantically through her bag as the disaster sirens wailed. She pulled out the notebook she'd written in while she waited in line on Distribution Day and couldn't help smiling at her angry scribbles. Yeah, she'd been pretty ticked that day. Then she spied her CSD on the dresser, and quickly squeezed out her dose.

I never did make it to my afternoon classes on Distribution Day, did I? I don't think I've been to class at all since... While she tried to remember, she ran her finger beneath the neckline of her shirt, tracing a cool line from her cleavage to her collarbone; the pleasant tingle left her breathless. *Who has time to study, anyway?* She tossed the notebook on the bed, took one of the lunch packets from her Essential Services delivery, and wandered out the door, bound for nowhere in particular.

Posters of the martyr were plastered on nearly every wall, tree, and fence in her neighborhood. Lips moving, she recited the mantra over and over as she walked. "Just when things were about to get better...for all of us." The corner news ticker ran the message "SID FRIEDMAN: MARTYR OR FOOL? FUNERAL COVERAGE BEGINS AT 10 AM EST. TAKE YOUR DAILY DOSE. IT'S A SMALL PRICE TO PAY FOR YOUR SAFETY."

Careen wandered past the university campus and into a trendy shopping district where a charming variety of expensive boutiques beckoned window-shoppers to step inside for a closer look. The setting was so perfectly OP-439, except that there were no chattering groups of students or expensively dressed housewives in the cafés or on the sidewalks. *Where was everyone?* There weren't many shopping centers left, and when people were about, being here was like watching a movie from an earlier time. She trailed her hand along a toy shop window and discovered that her fingers each wrote with a different color. She doodled a yellow sunshine—a circle with lines radiating outward, like a child's drawing. Warmth radiated from her little sun, and she drew a house by a lake and a boy in a boat. Tall grasses waved along the shore.

When she stepped back to look at her work, she heard a dripping sound. Color ran from her fingertips and puddled on the sidewalk, pooling around her until she was in the center of a huge artist's palette. She danced and spun through the rainbow of colors and flung handfuls of paint in joyous splatters on the shops, sidewalk, and the spindly tree trapped in its small square of dirt.

Then someone said her name. Startled, she turned and spattered the front of his uniform with paint. A quadrant marshal? She stood frozen, except for the drip-drip-drip of the paint.

"Careen, have you found what you're looking for?" His voice wasn't angry, just low and urgent. She studied his face. His brown eyes were deep-set under bushy eyebrows, and his wiry dark hair was unruly. The pink fog crept in at the edges of her vision, and she blushed when he didn't look away. *He's not much older than I am. I wonder what I'm looking for?* Then she heard her father say, "Tell me about what you're learning in school." She looked around and he was there, reflected in the shop window beside her. She smiled with relief. *Daddy. I've missed you.*

The marshal stepped closer and whispered a name in her ear, but it meant nothing to her.

Her father kissed the top of her head. "Don't forget, kiddo." Then she was alone on the sidewalk, splattered with paint. The disaster siren keened again, and the female voice spoke. "This is not a drill. Though toxins are present at lethal levels, taking the antidote will assure your safety."

There was a Help Wanted sign propped in a corner of the shop window. *I want help.* She pushed open the door and ran inside.

Careen caught sight of herself in a full-length mirror and, disbelieving, brushed her hand across her shirt. She was clean and dry. *Where did the paint go?* The paint was forgotten as soon as she noticed the boutique's tempting array of fall clothing and accessories, and she wandered happily through the racks. She stopped when she noticed a glass vial on a silver chain. She took it off the display to cradle it in her palm, and when she closed her fingers over it, the silver trim on the vial felt cool and substantial. *I could keep my dose in here and wear it; then I won't ever lose it. That'll help me be safe.* She hung the chain around her neck.

She wanted to pay for the necklace, but there was no clerk to be found. She looked in the rear of the shop, and decided to wait for an employee to return. Before long she was hungry, so she sat behind the counter and ate her lunch. Soon an expensively dressed older woman came in and began to browse through the sweaters. Careen quickly finished eating.

"Are you new, dear? I don't remember seeing you here before."

"Umm, yes." *Technically true.*

"It's positively shocking how many workers have become unreliable since this whole business started. I suppose they're afraid, but it's such an inconvenience!"

Careen smiled noncommittally as she swiped the woman's debit card through the reader and bagged her purchase. As she walked the woman to the door, she saw the marshal studying her through the window. *He might think I stole the necklace.* She turned away and tucked it inside the front of her shirt, then got her own debit card out of her bag. She considered putting the necklace back when she saw the price tag, but bought it anyway. *I need it. And I'm not a thief.*

She looked out the window and saw him across the street. He was pretending he wasn't watching her, but when she poked her head out the door, he darted in her direction. She slammed the door shut and grabbed a key hanging on the wall nearby. She heard the lock's tumblers fall into place just as he tried to push his way inside; his mouth twisted in anger and he slammed both palms against the door frame.

Careen snatched the key and ran behind the counter into a back room, dodging cardboard boxes and a rack of empty hangers as she looked for a way out. She opened the back door cautiously and peeked out into a small, dank alley, separated from the buildings behind it by a wooden fence that was too high to scale.

He could be waiting around either corner. She let the door close quietly and glanced both ways. Her first instinct was to seek safety at her apartment, but she darted down the alley in the opposite direction. She emerged on a side street and ran full-out to the next corner before ducking down another street lined with shops. She made random turns every few blocks and wished for crowds of people in which to lose herself. Soon she reached the edge of the shopping district and found herself in a neighborhood where the once stately hundred-year-old homes were showing their age. *Keep moving. Act natural.* Though there was no one about, Careen felt as if she were being watched from every window. *I wish I knew where I was.* She fought the urge to run, and looked around for anything familiar.

Lights twinkling in an upstairs window caught her eye and she remembered. *It's not Christmas.*

She broke into a run, tearing across the street to a Deco-style building where she pushed into the vestibule. In seconds she was pounding on the door of an upstairs apartment.

When he answered she shoved past him into the room and quickly locked the door, but she was so embarrassed by what she could recall of their last encounter that she couldn't look him in the eye. "I need help." She stared at the ground and tried to think over the thudding of her adrenaline-charged pulse. "Someone's following me, and I don't know why. Can I hide here?" She was breathing fast, alert to every sound, but he seemed completely unconcerned.

"Who?"

She looked up impatiently. "Who, what? Some quadrant marshal, but I don't know his name or why..."

"Yeah, okay." He smiled as he took a step toward her, put his hands at her waist and pulled her closer.

Against her will, the warm, comforting pink haze swam up to meet her again. Her heart was already pounding. It would be so easy to just give in to him. *But there's something I'm supposed to remember. And I'm pretty sure this isn't it.* She tried to pull away. "No, really, I just want to hide here for a while. I'll go as soon as it's safe." *Whenever that is.*

He kept his hands around her waist and walked her backward a few steps into the room.

"Look, never mind. I'll go." She pushed at his hands.

"Hey, baby. No worries. You can crash for a while." He stepped back, and gestured her grandly into his messy studio apartment. The martyr's funeral was playing on the television, and when he sat at one end of the sofa, she moved to the far end. They watched the graveside ceremony in silence.

The images in the safety video that followed frightened her, and she clutched at the vial around her neck. *It's the only way.* She got up and carried her messenger bag to the kitchen table. She glanced over her shoulder, but he didn't seem to be paying attention.

She found her antidote bottle deep in one of the side pockets of her bag and set it on the table, then unscrewed the top of her vial necklace. As she transferred the antidote from the dropper, a few drops fell on the tabletop. She wiped them up with her fingers and touched them to her tongue, loathe to waste any. She capped the glass vial, and the orange antidote glowed against her shirt where it hung between her breasts.

She began to feel safer almost immediately, as though the necklace were an ancient talisman that offered some kind of mystical protection.

PeopleCam began another re-broadcast of the funeral. Careen thought she should feel sad, but she didn't. She watched her host as he sat, mesmerized by the funeral.

It was getting dark, so she turned on all the lights, just like she did every evening at home. She didn't want to watch the funeral again. She picked up the remote and tried to shut off the television. *Shoot. Mandatory programming. Can I at least turn down the sound?* She pushed the down arrow key on the remote, and the screen itself got smaller and smaller, until it was just a tiny flickering square, and she breathed a sigh of relief. Still he stared at the screen. She stood in front of him to block his view. "Hey. Let's not watch anymore."

"Hmmm?" He tilted his head, looking around her.

"Don't you ever wonder?"

"Wonder what?"

"Wonder anything!"

He took her hand and pulled till she straddled his lap. "I was wondering when you were coming back."

5:25 PM

The streetlights came on, one by one, as Wes trudged back toward Careen's apartment, frustrated and perplexed. *Where the hell did she go, anyway?* He'd tried to intercept her as she fled the store, but by the time he'd run into the alley, she was gone. He couldn't believe she gave him the slip when she was high on CSD. When he'd seen her up close, she'd reminded him of Mitch: calm on the surface, but with little control over what she said or did. Gently, trying not to frighten her, he'd whispered, "Find Tom Bailey," to push her in the right direction. But he'd spooked her, and now he'd have to find another way to make her believe she needed to find Tom Bailey. He glanced around and, seeing no one, opened the door to her building and stepped inside.

Chapter 6

Madalyn Davies fumed at being treated like a babysitter. Dr. Stratford had insisted that she be the one to monitor Trina Jacobs as she sat slack jawed, slumped in a chair all day. Anyone could see Trina was no threat to the CSD project. Madalyn had demanded double overtime pay to come in on the weekend, which Stratford had rather rudely refused.

She was turning the key in the lock when Kevin McGraw came around the corner, pushing a nearly empty lab cart. He smiled and called, "Hey, Madalyn!"

Madalyn rolled her eyes. *Oh joy. My other favorite co-worker.* Kevin, a lab assistant, was a meek, bald, slightly built man who barely came up to her shoulder. He was friendly with everyone in the office, but she suspected his cheerfulness was all an act, and his real motive was to latch on to his more powerful co-workers. *He gives me the creeps.* She nodded coldly.

"Are you busy? The lab needs you to look at some formula analysis before they test the production sequences for Phase Two." She tried to slip into the office and block Trina from his view, but he followed her, file in hand, before she could protest. He gasped as he spied Trina lolling in her chair. "Is that Dr. Jacobs?"

Madalyn feigned concern. "We're still trying to get Dr. Jacobs' dosage right. It's been terrible." *She looks like hell, poor dear.* Trina's hair was matted and sticking up on one side, and her coffee-colored skin was dull and ashy. She wore a hospital gown, an old cardigan, and slippers.

Kevin crossed the room and stared down at Trina. "She looks awful. Is she going to be all right?"

"She'll be fine. Dr. Jacobs was part of our last trial group, and there are bound to be a few bugs to work out." Madalyn took the file from

Kevin, crossed to the door and held it open, leaving no doubt that he was being dismissed.

6:55 PM

Kevin shut off his computer, grabbed his jacket, and locked his office door. His basement office at OCSD headquarters was like having the worst table in a great restaurant. Years ago he'd taken this job hoping to become an important part of the OCSD team and move upstairs into one of the more luxurious offices, but that didn't seem likely to happen now. He'd come to terms with his role as a gofer. At least he was a gofer at the most influential government agency in the country.

At the moment he was looking forward to going home and seeing what had come in his Essential Services delivery. Corn chips would be really nice, though he didn't hold out much hope. He couldn't remember the last time he'd had junk food in his delivery.

He found the hallway blocked by several chairs and a crossed pair of mops. A hand-lettered sign indicated that the floor had been freshly waxed. He sighed and turned around, frustrated by the delay. As he headed out the other way, he passed an unfamiliar hallway, its door slightly ajar, and peered into the gloom. The corridor was lit only by dim emergency lights, spaced far apart. Curiosity got the better of him, and he slipped inside. His footsteps sounded disconcertingly loud in the semi-darkness, and he winced as he walked. A square of light shone through the window on one of the doors near the end of the hall. He glanced in as he passed then doubled back to stare at a large bald man who lay restrained in a hospital bed. Their eyes met, and the man thrashed and pulled against his shackles and let out a scream that, by all rights, should have penetrated the soundproof door. As they stared at each other, the intensity of the scream distorted the tattoo of the sun on the man's face into something barely recognizable.

That's the martyr! But he's supposed to be dead. I watched his funeral three times. Completely rattled, Kevin fled back to the familiarity of the main hallway and took the long way out of the building.

There were no corn chips in his delivery. Kevin watched the rebroadcast of Sid Friedman's funeral while he ate dinner, looking for anything that would indicate that maybe, just maybe, someone else knew the man being honored as a martyr was still alive.

Everyone seemed to believe Sid Friedman was dead. He'd been buried with military honors. The president and the first lady had laid a wreath at his grave. Vendors were selling martyr sweatshirts, for crying out loud! Kevin had seen dozens of posters with Friedman's face and the slogan of the day plastered on nearly every fence and shop window on his way home. Could he be wrong about what he thought he saw?

That night he tossed and turned, unable to sleep. The martyr was locked in a room right down the hall from his office! He wished there were someone he could talk to.

Chapter 7

9:02 AM
Day 8: Friday, November 3, 2034
Quadrant OP-439

Careen went from deep sleep to wide-awake in an instant. Her fingers were working furiously, clawing her way toward daylight. She breathed a sigh of relief. It was morning. *The dark didn't catch me.*

She heard the shower running. The other half of the bed was empty, so she rolled over into the warmth he'd left behind and buried her face in his pillow. Her fingers found the vial on the chain around her neck.

Three drops into a half-empty soda can. *Breakfast of champions,* she thought as she drank. Soon the can began licking her fingers, and she tossed it into the trash.

She leaned back against the pillows, looking at her hands, and watched sunlight play on her rings. When she held up her fingers, rivulets of sunlight ran down toward her wrist. When she flipped her wrist down, the light dripped off her nails.

The sound of the shower stopped and he returned dressed in sweatpants, drying his hair with a towel. She held up the vial, opened it with a flourish, and poured three more drops on her tongue.

11:02 AM

Careen stumbled into the bathroom. *Wow. I look terrible with bed head.* Not that it mattered, really. She smiled, and a glint of sunlight shone from between her teeth. She licked her fingers and combed them through her hair. *Instant highlights.* In the shower, the water ran pink and smelled of roses, and her new highlights dried the color of a sunset. *Red sky at night...sailor's delight. Yep. That's me.*

She dressed in yesterday's clothes and tiptoed across the room, pausing with her hand on the doorknob. He was snoring softly, and she felt no need to wake him to say goodbye. Outside, she shivered as she hurried down the sidewalk. The temperature had dropped overnight, and her breath froze in the air, enveloping her in a crystalline pink haze. *Who am I looking for? No...who is looking for* me*?* Though she formed the thoughts without emotion, she still glanced over her shoulder every few seconds because she knew the pink haze did not conceal her.

About a quarter mile from her apartment, she heard hoarse shouts, almost like crying, coming from inside a white house on a corner. She couldn't remember the last time she'd cried. Curious, she crept onto the wide front porch, peered in a window, and saw a blond boy about her age limping around the living room, waving an empty milk carton.

After a while, the boy knelt awkwardly at the bottom of the stairs in the front hall, and she watched as he brushed his hand across his parents' gravestone. His head bowed, and his fingers pressed into the words engraved there: **Beloved Mother and Father**.

11:49 AM

Tommy had flopped on the couch and dozed off after his morning workout, too exhausted to shower. He slept until the television powered up and the announcer's voice filled the room.

"Detectible toxin levels up to vomiting have been recorded on the East Coast, with mostly dizziness levels over the Rockies and into the Southwest. It looks like things are gearing up to get worse, folks. We may have big changes in your local DTLs by the weekend."

He sat up, rubbing his eyes, and reached for his bottle. He had no idea how much time CSD needed to work, but once there were toxin levels in the air around him it was probably too late. He hurried upstairs and stood in the shower far longer than usual, just in case. Afterward, he ignored the weights and therapy band lying in the middle of the living room floor, changed the channel to VacationCam, and dozed off again while watching *Driving Through the Dutch Countryside*.

When he opened his eyes, he was lying on a picnic blanket, surrounded by tall grass. The sun was warm overhead, and the air smelled sweet.

"Tommy? You forgot to water the grass!"

"Mom?" He jumped to his feet but couldn't see his mother. Grass carpeted the living room, and tiny shoots were sprouting on the stairs; but he'd neglected to care for it, and some of it was turning brown. He grabbed a watering can and broke a path across the room, sprinkling sparkling drops over the parched grass. *I can't let it die. I can't.* But the delicate blades turned brittle as the water fell upon them. "Mom, I won't let it die! I promise," he shouted, flinging water in wide arcs across the room, but the grass sank and shriveled around him. Over in the corner by the stairs, a red rose sprang from the cracked soil and began to twist itself around the banister. Tommy scuffed through the tangled grass until he was close enough to see the engraving on the bottom step: **Beloved Mother and Father**.

He sank to his knees and ran his hands over the step, brushing the dead grass off his parents' gravestone.

12:00 PM

Careen completed the slow trek back to her apartment. The blond boy's despair had seeped in through the protective haze of pink around her, and she was plagued by grief so palpable that she could see it rising and rushing toward her like an incoming tide.

At home, her unmade bed bothered her. The rumpled covers signaled that she was losing focus and that things were spiraling out of control. She picked up her old, battered, stuffed cat, the only relic of her childhood that she'd brought to college with her, and shook out the comforter. Her notebook fell to the floor, and she picked it up, but as she tried to read, the words swirled into a vortex. They were being sucked away, down the drain, one at a time. Careen shook the notebook in frustration, and as the words bounced back to their places on the page, she scanned the entries.

Been waiting in this stupid, stupid line forever. The distribution center is run by a couple of completely incompetent old ladies and policed by security guards that beat you and drag you out to goodness knows where just for asking a question. Shouldn't we be able to get more information before we take the antidote? We have no say in the matter. That's what they mean by a small price, I guess.

The next entry was five days later.

I think I was followed. No contact this time. Too dangerous. He was waiting outside when I came home but I pretended I didn't see him. Won't give up.

Her handwriting was messier in the later entry; once the words had just trailed off the edge of the page. Careen shook her head in disbelief. *I don't remember that. Who am I trying to contact and why? And who is following me?* She shuddered.

Chapter 8

7:45 AM
Day 11: Monday, November 6, 2034
Quadrant DC-001

Madalyn stood to the side as Dr. Stratford swiped his ID through the reader and pressed his thumb on the scanner. The door to Trina's lab slid open, and Madalyn took a step back at the recorded chorus of shouting, crying people calling out from within.

Stratford chuckled. "Go on—they won't bite. Once you make sure there's nothing in here Dr. Jacobs can use to counteract our progress in Phase One, we can regulate her dose so she's less catatonic and just keep her in here during the day. It'll make things look more… normal."

She obediently stepped inside, and the door slid shut. *I don't know what he expects me to find.* She glanced around the room. The space was spotless and nearly devoid of personal items; there was just one photo of Dr. Jacobs, in her graduation cap and gown, surrounded by family. Her purse and briefcase lay on the credenza. Madalyn looked through both, but noticed nothing interesting.

Then she saw the green light on the desktop monitor, and tapped the mouse to wake up the computer. An open file displayed the lab results from Trina's last attempt at an antidote. Madalyn quickly read the results. "Oh my, Dr. Jacobs! What were you up to, anyway?"

8:53 AM

Trina opened a file on her computer to retrieve the lab results from the day before.

GAME OVER flashed on the screen in red letters. "What? I've got one more turn left." She hit the Escape key over and over.

Dr. Stratford's face appeared on the screen. "Apparently you lack the essential qualities to win this game, Dr. Jacobs. I'll be moving on to the championship round without you." He motioned to his right. The shot on the computer monitor widened to reveal the president standing beside Stratford. The two men shook hands, and Trina heard applause.

Then her eyes flew open. She remembered everything. She breathed rapidly, trying not to panic. *How much time before they come in and dose me?* She had to get out of there and stop Stratford, but every new dose of CSD rendered her completely helpless.

She didn't resist when the lab tech administered her dose, but inside she was fighting to stay focused, mentally sinking her teeth in and hanging on. She could out-think Stratford, even on that Crazy-Slow-Me-Down drug of his.

As the lab tech walked her down the hall, the floor tiles shifted randomly under her feet. *Stripes*, she commanded, and they obeyed. Her eyes narrowed. *Checkerboard.* They leapt to her bidding. *Plaid*, she countered. The tiles shuddered, shifted, and stopped in disarray, defeated.

Trina smiled knowingly as her escort pressed her thumb to the scanner outside her lab door. *There's one thing Stratford didn't bargain for. I always win in the end. Always.*

1:37 PM

Kevin rounded a corner in the third-floor hallway and nearly collided with a janitor. The young man met Kevin's gaze for a moment, then dropped his eyes and resumed his placid mopping. *I bet he never hurries.* Kevin jumped and hopped down the hall on tiptoe, trying to minimize where he stepped on the wet floor.

He tapped on a door and stuck his head inside. "Madalyn? The lab still needs you to authorize the first run on the Phase Two formulas. And I brought you a piece of the peach cobbler they've got in the lunchroom. Brought one for Trina, too." Kevin held up two plates so she could see them.

"Come in." She sat in a chair across the room from Trina, filing her nails.

He pushed open the door with his shoulder and set one of the plates down beside her, before sneaking a peek at Trina, who looked better than the last time he'd seen her. Today she was dressed in a sweater and slacks, and her hair was combed. Her eyes were still unfocused, but when the computer screen flashed CLICK NOW, her finger tapped the mouse.

"Dr. Jacobs? Would you like some cobbler?" He looked back at Madalyn. "I don't think she's eating enough." He brought a forkful up to Trina's mouth. "Just a little?"

She opened her mouth and took the bite. As she chewed, a tear slid from the corner of her eye. He pulled up a chair and sat beside her.

"Um, Madalyn, I'm gonna stay and help her finish this. I'm still on my lunch break. You wanna get out of here for a bit?"

"With pleasure." She swept out the door.

He speared a peach with the fork and leaned in close. "Hang in there, Trina," he whispered.

Chapter 9

Careen cowered in her bed, reading and rereading a message that was scrawled on her forearm with a Sharpie. The nagging thought of something important left undone had been present each morning when she woke up, but always faded after she took her dose. At first she thought she'd written the message herself, and she'd freaked out when she realized it was on her left arm—and she was left-handed. She'd grabbed a pen and tried to write on herself using her right hand, but the result was unreadable. Someone else had written GET ANSWERS, followed by an address, on her arm. She had no idea who'd written it, no clue what it meant, and no recollection of when or where she'd received it. None.

She took her dose, and when she noticed the message again a few minutes later, she felt none of the panic that had plagued her before. Instead, she calmly mapped the address on her phone and set out. Before long she was in a nice residential neighborhood, and she recognized the house to which she'd been directed. *The guy with the milk lives there. Do I make contact with* him? *But how? What do I want to know?* Stalling, she strolled around the block and approached again, wishing the hedges that bordered the driveway were high enough to conceal her. She self-consciously ran her fingers through her bangs, and wished she could settle the fluttering in her stomach.

Then she heard the side door slam, and he came down the steps, carrying a pair of crutches. *Crutches...I should remember something about crutches.* He shot her a crooked half smile as he tossed them into a trashcan, and she slowed her pace and smiled back. There was a golden glow about him that was almost as nice as pink. *Making contact with him wouldn't be so bad. Not bad at all.*

"Well, look at you, up and around!"

He looked over his shoulder and Careen watched woman in a fashionable dress and boots hurry up the driveway toward him, arms outstretched. She gathered him close and kissed his cheek, clinging to him.

Careen retreated, unsure what to do. When she looked back, they seemed to be engrossed in conversation, so she circled the block again. This time as she approached, she saw a gray-haired man in a suit slip out the back door and glance over his shoulder as he hurried through the gate. She ducked behind the garage so he wouldn't see her. *Sheesh. Maybe I haven't been able to make contact because it's too busy around here.*

When she was sure the gray-haired man had gone, she walked by the house again, looking for the young guy, but she didn't see him. She was too nervous to knock on the door. *How many times have I tried and failed already? Are the answers for myself, or someone else? Is someone watching me right now?* Her stomach lurched in fear and she fled.

9:53 AM

Tommy stepped out of the shower and toweled off, then threw on a faded pair of jeans and a sweatshirt. He'd gone to work out at the high school track for the last four mornings in a row, and he was feeling stronger. His speed was coming back, little by little, and he no longer had to cling to the railing on his way down the stairs. Even though he knew he shouldn't, he held off taking his dose because he didn't want to cut short his endorphin rush.

From the kitchen window, he saw a cute girl about his age walking down the sidewalk on the other side of the hedges. She looked familiar, but he couldn't seem to place her. The wind ruffled her dark brown bangs and she combed them back into place with her fingers. She was slender, but he could tell by the way her sweater clung to her curves that she was definitely…squeezable. *Today's a good day for new beginnings.* He noticed the crutches leaning against the wall, grabbed them and carried them outside. He wanted people to see him as whole. *I want her to see me…*He smiled at her and was encouraged when she smiled back. He pointedly tossed the crutches in the trash.

"Well, look at you, up and around!"

He turned, startled.

Beth Severson hurried toward him, arms extended, and planted a kiss on his cheek. "We hadn't heard from you in a while, Tommy. Thought I'd better stop by and check on you."

"I'm fine." He returned the hug, glancing over Beth's shoulder toward the sidewalk. The girl was gone.

"Art and I want you to come over for dinner sometime this week. Maybe stay and watch a ball game or some VacationCam?"

"Okay."

"Have you thought any more about college?"

"Not yet."

"I don't want to push, honey, but you could still enroll for next semester. Your mom and dad would have wanted you to go."

"Yeah, they would." He turned to go back inside.

"Tommy." Her voice broke. "I miss them, too. I miss your mom. We said goodbye that night, and I didn't think it was…goodbye, you know? I still can't believe they're dead. But you're here. And I can be here for you. So, please…let me." A tear rolled down her cheek.

He sighed. "Yeah, okay. I'll come over soon. Thanks for checking on me." He walked her to her car at the end of the driveway. Back in the house, he shut the door quietly, deliberately, then picked up a vase off the hall table and flung it against the wall. It felt great, but it wasn't nearly enough. He stepped into the living room, grabbed a porcelain statue off the mantel and watched it explode against the hearth, then darted through the house, smashing at random, until shards of pottery and glass crunched beneath his feet.

You're my bull in a china shop, Tommy. It was his mom's voice inside his head. He didn't feel like a bull. He felt dizzy and weak as he sank into a chair at the kitchen table. He took his three drops, buried his face in his arms, and sobbed.

11:30 AM

Careen felt sure someone was following her, but every time she turned around, she was alone on the street. Going home was out of the question, and she had only one other haven.

Soon she was climbing the stairs to his apartment. The door was unlocked, and she slipped inside. He was still asleep so she curled up on the sofa and pushed up the sleeve of her sweater to stare at the unfamiliar handwriting there. *Answers. What do I know for sure? Nothing...*

The door flew open with a bang, and she cowered as two quadrant marshals strode into the apartment. They yanked her companion out of bed and in seconds had his hands cuffed behind his back. *They should let him put on a shirt and shoes, shouldn't they?* She felt like she was watching the arrest on TV, until one of the marshals started toward her.

"What about this one?"

She shrank back against the sofa cushion.

"She's not on our list." The second marshal's voice sounded familiar. Careen looked at him, and for some reason she thought of brightly colored paints. His gaze flickered over her as she cowered, arms clutched in front of her, and lingered on her face for a moment too long. She dropped her eyes.

"Arresting one enemy of the state is a good day's work. Right?"

The marshals dragged him from the apartment and were gone before she realized no one had asked her name. *He didn't ask because I think he knows me. How does that marshal know who I am?*

She watched from the window as they loaded him into a Jeep and drove away; then she ran, keeping to the side streets and alleys, all the way back to her apartment. The marshal had called him an enemy of the state. What did that mean, exactly? As far as she knew he could barely form a cohesive thought. How could he be dangerous? Was he a spy? He'd once flirted with her in class, and he'd been waiting when she came out of the distribution center. Had he sought her out on purpose? Had they shared secrets she couldn't remember? Outside her apartment, she glanced around warily before she let herself in, but saw no one. She turned on the television and all the lights before crawling into bed fully clothed, shivering despite the thick down comforter she'd pulled over her head, convinced there were threats lurking that were more dangerous than the toxins in the air.

12:36 PM

Wes Carraway shut the cell door and walked back to his desk. He felt a twinge of guilt, arresting that poor guy for no reason, but taking him out of the equation was the easiest way to keep Careen on track. The writ of *habeus corpus* and Miranda rights had been eliminated years ago, so that kid would stay locked up indefinitely while the quadrant marshals searched for evidence to build a case against him. Or not.

On the other hand, he felt no guilt about lying to his partner about Careen's name being on the warrant list, even though they should have arrested her instead of her friend. She'd failed her CSD check-in four days in a row, but he was doing everything he could to keep her away from the QM. That girl had a way of attracting attention. As a matter of fact, she constantly occupied his own thoughts.

He'd been working long shifts and spending his off-duty hours tailing her, and he was getting impatient. She was being too coy about making contact with the suspected terrorist. The day she'd run away from him, he'd taken matters into his own hands when he jimmied the door to her place and forged an entry in her journal.

It had been so easy to break in to her apartment. The hard part was staying away. Every time he went there, he told himself it was okay to protect her and watch over her while she slept. And so he'd just watched her sleep…until last night. Now he couldn't forget the scent of her tousled hair on the pillow and the feel of her warm, soft skin where he'd written the clue. It had taken all his resolve not to join her under the covers.

Now that her name was on the warrant list, he wouldn't be the only QM who was interested in her. He had to stay focused on the mission.

Chapter 10

Day 13: Wednesday, November 8, 2034

The Washington Post
Editorial Page

Three Cheers for the Government!
I raise my dose of CSD in a toast to the Office of Civilian Safety and Defense, and especially to Dr. Lowell Stratford, the visionary who conceived, developed, and perfected the antidote to chemical warfare. We have survived one nationwide chemical attack and several regional ones so far, and we will prevail against terrorism!

My fellow Americans, after years of worrying about terrorist threats, we can rest easy. The Office of Civilian Safety and Defense has proved it can, and will, protect the American people from our enemies. It's been nearly two weeks since we began using CSD, and frankly, I have never felt better! Apparently I am not alone. The nation's crime rate has declined sixty-five percent, and early indicators confirm the economy is stabilizing, due in part to the creation of new jobs in the medical field and in CSD distribution.

With compassion for all who occupy American soil, your benevolent government continues to provide CSD free of charge, not only to American citizens but to illegal immigrants as well. Even our huddled masses need not cower before this threat.

Kevin's office door was standing open when he arrived at work. He felt a jolt of fear and slowed his pace as he tiptoed up to the door. The lights were on, but he couldn't see inside. He took a deep breath and, intending to surprise whoever was in there, leaped through the doorway, ninja-style.

A janitor was on a ladder, his head and shoulders inside the drop ceiling. He didn't see Kevin, who edged into his office, feeling more than a little foolish.

The janitor descended the ladder and quietly closed the door. When he turned around, there was nothing lazy about the expression on his face. He looked Kevin in the eyes and spoke rapidly.

"I just disconnected your monitor, but at best that's only good for a few minutes of guaranteed privacy. You know what's going on, don't you?"

Kevin stared at him, not sure how to respond.

"Come on! You know the OCSD has doped most everyone in the country in the name of safety. They've all been doped and duped, man, because this terrorist threat is a complete fabrication. I've been watching you and you're more human than most people around here. You visit Dr. Jacobs every day. Doesn't it bother you what they've done to her?"

Kevin felt sick to his stomach. Last week he'd convinced himself that the OCSD must have a good reason for keeping Sid Friedman locked up in the basement. He'd believed Madalyn's explanation that Trina had experienced a bad reaction to CSD. Even if there were cover-ups happening at OCSD, his employers wouldn't lie about something as important as a terrorist attack. Would they?

"Well, sure. I mean, Trina's my friend. But…" he hung his head.

"We're fighting back—and we need you, man." The janitor slipped a folded piece of paper into Kevin's shirt pocket and climbed back up the ladder.

"Wait. Who's we?"

"The *real* good guys. Duh." He reconnected the television, replaced the ceiling tile, and climbed down. Folding his ladder, he winked at Kevin and left, leaving the door open.

When Kevin saw Madalyn standing over Trina, dropper in hand, he was flooded with a rage unlike anything he'd ever felt. But if there was anything different in his demeanor, Madalyn didn't seem to notice.

"Oh, good, you're here. I've been trying to dose her, but she's getting stronger and I can't make her sit still." She gripped Trina's shoulder as Trina twisted away, mouth clamped shut.

"Give me the bottle, Madalyn." He spoke with authority, ready to take it from her if necessary, but Madalyn surrendered it eagerly and was out the door before he finished speaking. He bent close to Trina, facing away from the monitor just in case Stratford was watching, and whispered, "Trina, do you understand me?"

She didn't react. He opened the bottle and squeezed the dropper.

She rolled her eyes toward him and gave him a don't-even-think-about-it look. Her voice was raspy, barely audible. "Dose me with that shit and I will kick your skinny white butt."

That sounded like the Dr. Jacobs he knew. "What's wrong with you? Why does CSD affect you that way?"

She moistened her lips and swallowed. "You're all on…a placebo. I'm not. Stratford doped me to shut me up. Now they've reduced my dose and I can…hold it off for a while. But it always catches up with me. I need a day off that stuff to get my brain back. But Stratford and Madalyn can't know."

He struggled to comprehend. "What do you mean, placebo? I'm on a placebo? If there's another attack, everyone who's not taking the real antidote could be in danger."

She shook her head and whispered, "It's fake. All of it. Government workers think they're on a…miracle antidote. Nothing but sugar water. Meanwhile Stratford's gotten the rest of the country high."

"But why? Why would he do that?"

"Get control of their minds so they'll believe anything he tells them."

"I think they already do." Whispering, he told her about the martyr.

12:10 PM

Kevin waited until he was alone in his office to look at the slip of paper. It contained a phone number and a message: *password* MENO CIBU RDA *to Jeff*. "What am I supposed to do with this?" He stuffed the paper back into his pocket.

During his lunch break, Kevin left the building, and when he was a couple blocks away he pulled the paper out and looked at it again. Even after what he'd learned from Trina and the janitor, he couldn't help wondering if this was a trap to gauge his loyalty to the OCSD. Intrigue and savvy were not in his skill set.

He decided to send the message. If he got a response that seemed off, he could toss his phone on the side of the road and say he lost it. Then it could've been anyone who sent the message. Pretty flimsy, but it was the only plan he had. He keyed in the nonsense syllables and hit Send before he could change his mind. Three minutes later, his phone beeped. He opened the message with shaking hands and read, *Hi, Kevin. This is Jeff. I hear you're our new inside guy.*

What? Who are you? He closed his eyes for a moment before hitting the Send button. He knew this was the point of no return.

Best we meet in person someplace we can talk freely. Saturday 10 AM. There was an address, in a quadrant that was five, maybe six, hours away. Kevin's heart sank. As an OCSD employee, he was allowed to own a personal car, but he rarely drove farther than the few miles to work and back.

Another message pinged. *Not to sound clichéd, but come alone, Kevin—or we'll know, and then we'll be forced to kill you. Best, Jeff.*

Fantastic. Kevin couldn't believe he was actually considering such a reckless rendezvous.

2:27 PM

Trina stared benignly at the solitaire game on her computer screen, but inside she was anything but calm. She should be saving the world, or at least saving herself, yet she spent day after day playing the biggest time-waster on the planet.

Madalyn sat nearby, flipping through a magazine on her tablet. Her constant presence gave Trina the fidgets. How could she plot against th OCSD in front of Miss Tattletale?

Early that morning, before Madalyn arrived at work, Trina had logged on and searched the OCSD lab files for anything that would give her an idea what Stratford was planning to do next. She realized his plan went beyond merely controlling people with the Phase One formula. She'd found that interoffice memo she'd hurriedly skimmed back in October, then dug around in his files and downloaded a document on the project, but hadn't had time to read it. If it contained what she thought it did, she was going to need a chance to read it carefully.

She longed to overpower Madalyn and make her escape, but she had to wait until the time was right. Otherwise Stratford and Madalyn would lock her up in the makeshift loony ward with that martyr guy. She suppressed a shudder and clicked the mouse.

2:55 PM

Kevin stopped by the cafeteria and delivered the last of the morning's sweet rolls to Trina's office prison. Madalyn, conditioned to take a break whenever Kevin arrived, leapt up at the sight of him and hurried out of the room without a word. He set the plate on the desk and looked down at Trina. She glanced his way and winked.

Kevin didn't waste any time. "I know this guy who has a plan to sabotage the CSD formulas. I think I should try to help him, but I don't know enough about the procedures or formulas or anything. I don't know where to start."

Trina clicked the mouse and a file came up on the screen. He read the first few sentences "Holy Mother! Where did you get that?" He continued to read over her shoulder.

She slipped him a computer disc about the size of a quarter, which he tucked safely into his pocket. "You're the greatest," he murmured.

"You better believe it."

Trina's lips barely moved as she read quietly from the computer screen. "Increasing the level of scopolamine in Phase Two heightens the suggestibility factor." She paused. "That's good. We can use that."

Kevin sipped his coffee and avoided her gaze.

"You need to dose me with Phase Two in front of Madalyn on Friday. It'll make me into a good little worker bee."

"I think it would take more than Phase Two to make you into a good little worker bee."

She didn't change her expression or the tone of her voice. "Dose me in front of Madalyn, or I'll make good on my threat to kick your skinny white butt. It's the best way to get me into Stratford's inner circle."

The door opened behind them. He glanced over his shoulder and broke out in a cold sweat. It was Madalyn. Trina slid the mouse to the left and bumped it under his hand.

He looked back at the screen and was startled to see a game of solitaire. He moved the mouse, shifted a column, and the logjam broke. The cards flew to the top of the screen, then into the waterfall cascade that signaled a win.

"Isn't that cheating?" Madalyn smirked, arms crossed. She picked up a sweet roll and took a bite. "You're helping her."

Kevin shrugged. "Like she's gonna know."

He watched Trina's hand tremble on the mouse. He swallowed hard and kept his expression blank. *I'm figuring out how to play this game, and together, Trina and I are on our way to a win.*

Later that night, Kevin downloaded the file from the chip drive to his personal tablet and studied it carefully. What he read about the properties and intended uses of CSD's Phases One, Two and Three convinced him that helping the Resistance wasn't just the right thing to do—it was the only thing.

Chapter 11

2:45 AM
Day 15: Friday, November 10, 2034
Quadrant OP-439

Careen's heart pounded and she tried to relax as she leaned back against the dark wood paneling of the booth, nervously picking at lint on her sleeve. She couldn't wait to see him, and yet dreaded it at the same time. Even though the pub was dimly lit and all but empty, she felt like she was on display and exposed as she waited.

He opened the heavy wooden door and for a moment he was silhouetted in a rectangle of golden light. Then the door swung shut and he stepped into the semi-darkness, but the glow seemed to cling to him as he crossed the room and slid into the booth with her. He barely glanced her way, but he put his arm around her as though they knew each other well. Pressed close to his side, she felt safe. Loved. She leaned her head against his shoulder. "Hey."

"Yeah. Hey."

They sat without speaking for a full minute. When he slowly turned his gaze to hers, his blue eyes were deep and serious. She lifted her face in anticipation of a kiss, but instead of leaning closer, he whispered, "I don't know what's real anymore."

Careen awoke with a start. Panic pressed close around her. She threw back the covers and ran into the bathroom.

She gripped the sides of the sink and studied herself in the mirror. There were dark circles under her eyes, and the pink highlights had faded from her hair. Her knees were shaking. "I don't know what's real anymore." As soon as the words were out, her tears flowed hot, running down her cheeks and dripping into the sink.

2:45 AM

Fallen leaves scuttled across the sidewalk as Tommy rounded the corner toward his house. He hunched his shoulders against the chilly breeze and dug his hands deeper into his front pockets.

Even from half a block away, the front of the house looked shabby, like it could use a fresh coat of paint. But his dad always took care of stuff like that. Tommy had no idea if there was other home maintenance he ought to be doing. Did it matter? He was the only one who lived there. Sometimes he felt like he was the only one who lived, period.

But as he turned into the yard the front door opened, and the girl he'd seen the other day, the one with the long brown bangs, stepped out onto the porch. She smiled, and, trying to be cool, he resisted the urge to turn and look behind him.

She met him at the edge of the porch, and Tommy stopped one step below the top so they could see eye-to-eye. Hers were brown, just a shade lighter than her hair, with tiny flecks of gold in the irises. She smiled as she reached out and laced her fingers through his, and as she pulled him closer, everything came into sharp focus. "I've been waiting for you."

"I've been waiting for you, too." Tommy spoke aloud into the darkness, waking himself up.

6:26 AM

Careen huddled in the bathroom until it was almost daylight, then threw on a pair of jeans and a sweater, grabbed her messenger bag, and left. The streetlights were on, but as she hurried down the sidewalk, the patches of yellow light faded and went out. The sky glowed orange in front of her as the sun peeked over the horizon.

When she got to his house, she crept up the front steps and peered in the window, as she had done the day before. It was dark inside. Her vial necklace swung free and clicked against the window, and she impatiently tucked it inside the front of her sweater. *Not now. I'll take it later.*

She should just walk through the front door and find him, talk to him, but that sounded a lot easier than it was. She felt the same mixture of longing and dread she'd experienced in the dream, and pressed her palms against the screen door. The mesh of the screen pulsed softly, like a heartbeat.

Then the front door opened.

Careen stared up at him. His blue eyes widened and for a second she wanted to laugh because their bewildered expressions had to be mirrored in each other's faces.

"Do I know you?"

"I've been waiting for you," she said, thinking even as she spoke that it wasn't really an answer.

He flinched and stared at her as if she was crazy. Then he looked her up and down, opened the door, and pulled her into the house.

Startled, she looked behind her, but there wasn't anything there. The boy gave off a faint golden glow in the dim hallway, and she scanned his face as though she needed to commit it to memory. His left eye fixed her with an intense, open gaze; but his right eye, just a bit more heavy-lidded, maintained a hint of a wink that was laid-back and sexy. There was a recently-healed scar along his left jawbone, and when her eyes flickered to it, he looked away self-consciously. He was dressed in sweats and his blond hair was messy. He was a little bit of everything.

"I was going out for a run." He hesitated. "How did you…I mean, why are you here?"

"I've seen you a couple of times, and I had a dream about you last night. So I kind of came back to find you because I need *answers*."

"Yeah?"

Apparently "answers" isn't the password. Now what? "Yeah. And you're glowing, just like in my dream."

"Seriously?" He dubiously checked his reflection in the hall mirror. "I see some pretty freaky stuff, but I definitely don't see myself glowing."

"What kinds of things do you see?"

"Well for starters, how about those vines that were growing all over you when you were out on the porch? Grass grows inside the house, and sometimes it rains in here, too."

She tried to hide her confusion. Could this really be the guy she was supposed to contact?

After a long, uncomfortable silence, he asked, "Want some breakfast?"

Chapter 12

8:37 AM
Quadrant DC-001

Madalyn walked in just in time to see Kevin pull the empty dropper out of Trina's mouth. Trina's eyes fluttered and closed, and she slumped across her desk.

Kevin jumped back, flapping his hands in distress. "Is she okay? Did I do something wrong?"

"No, we're stepping up her dosage today. Remember, we had to reduce it a couple weeks ago? We're just now getting her back up to the recommended level."

He looked relieved. "Oh, okay. I was worried for a minute there." He took a stack of files off a lab cart. "I've got some authorizations for you. Dr. Stratford didn't have time, and he wants you to handle them." He pushed the cart toward the door, then turned back to look at her. "Gee, Madalyn, you're always so busy. It's too bad you don't have an assistant."

She watched him leave and returned her attention to Trina.

9:03 AM

Dr. Stratford held the door as Madalyn stepped into the elevator. "Another one? They're stacking up like cordwood!"

He shrugged. "There's nothing we can do about that. We've got to keep them somewhere, and it's best if we're the ones that monitor them."

The elevator stopped on the first level, and they crossed the lobby to a back entrance. Out in the parking lot, two ambulance attendants unloaded a gurney and wheeled it toward the door.

Madalyn whispered, "What's this guy's story?"

"Some big-mouthed college professor who made such a fuss about refusing to take his dose that his family called the QM to collect him.

He's been hospitalized for two weeks so they could treat him for a rare form of CSD-induced dementia, but he's failed to improve. That's because he doesn't want to. Now we'll see if we can't adjust his attitude."

The attendants brought the gurney into the lobby, and shook hands with Dr. Stratford. Madalyn signed off on transfer papers from a regional hospital in IN-546.

Stratford smiled and gave the attendants a thumbs-up. "I'm taking personal charge of this gentleman's care. Thank you for bringing him here." When the attendants were out of earshot, he turned to her. "Let's put him with the others."

They rode the elevator down to the basement, and he pushed the gurney past Kevin's office.

That reminded her of her new idea. "What are we going to do with Trina?"

"As long as she behaves, let's just let her run loose during the day and lock her in at night. It looks less suspicious if she's visible."

"I can make her my assistant. I need someone to help with my work, and now that she's on Phase Two, she'll do exactly what I tell her!"

Stratford seemed to like the idea. He swiped his ID in the card reader, opened the door, and together they rolled the gurney into the secure ward.

Chapter 13

There was no milk so Tommy and Careen sat on the living room sofa sharing cereal straight out of the box. She took a handful. "This is nice. I wasn't expecting to spend my day like this."

"What do you usually do?"

She thought for a moment before she replied. It was easier to remember things before she took her dose, but even though she was relatively clear-headed at the moment, she wasn't used to making conversation. "I'm not sure. I came here to go to the university, but I haven't been to class since, well, you know. Do you go to the university?"

"Nah. I was accepted, but now I have the money from my parents' life insurance, and I figured, why bother with more school."

"When did your parents die?"

"Last summer. Car accident."

"Wow! That's unusual, isn't it? I don't even know anyone who has a car." She paused again. "I'm really sorry about your parents. I lost my dad in a bombing when I was nine. Pretty much everybody I knew at home had buried somebody."

"Guess so. I don't see other people much."

"What *do* you do?"

"It's gonna sound weird, but when I work out, I try to outrun the grass. Sometimes I can."

"Yeah? With me, colors come right out of my fingers. But it's as if that's not even strange, you know?"

"Nothing surprises me anymore."

"Me either. See this?" Careen licked her fingers and trailed them through her bangs.

"No. What did you do?"

"Pink highlights."

She licked her finger again and lightly pressed the tip of his nose.

"*That* better not be pink." He rubbed his nose with the back of his hand. She smiled and shrugged.

The poison drill sirens began to howl in the distance. Careen grabbed for the vial around her neck and tipped it to her open mouth, but it was empty.

"You haven't taken yours today, either? Are you out?" He leapt off the couch and, leaning heavily on the railing, hurried up the stairs. He came back with his bottle. "There's only one dose left." He held the bottle up to the light and squinted. "We can split it for now."

She held out her finger, and he carefully squeezed one large drop for each of them. She mumbled a thank-you past her index finger, which she'd caught between her teeth. The sirens stopped, and the loudspeakers blared. "This is not a drill. Deadly levels of toxins are present in this quadrant."

She looked around as if for someplace to hide. "We'd better stay inside. Neither of us took a full dose. It'll help, staying inside, right?" She spoke faster as her panic accelerated.

"Sure," he said, but he sounded like he wasn't. "Looks like we might be hanging out for a while. Think maybe you could at least tell me your name?"

She glanced up at him. In those few moments, her anxiety had started to fade, and she was breathing more slowly as the mini-dose took effect. She tossed her head coquettishly and turned away. "Use your best pickup line, and maybe I'll tell you."

He came up behind her and bent close to her ear. "Hi, my name's Tommy. What's yours?"

Tommy. His voice sent a pleasant shiver up her spine. She lowered her head, but she knew he could see her smiling. Then she leaned back against him, and her head fit perfectly under his chin. "I'm Careen." It sounded like a sigh.

9:01 AM

Eduardo Rodriguez awoke to the same disaster alert siren he heard every single morning. "This is not a drill," intoned the female voice on the loudspeaker.

He groaned and pulled the pillow over his head. "Not again!"

I'm sick.

His conscience answered immediately. "No, you're not...not really."

Oh, God. Why me?

"You have to be strong."

But why? I'm sick of risking my life for people I don't even know. I only know their names and what their front doors look like.

"Pull it together and do your job. Just go."

Eduardo rolled out of bed and stumped to the kitchen. He poured himself a cup of coffee, mixed in Kahlúa and his last dose of CSD, and slurped it down. The concoction failed to quell his fears, and his left eyelid began to twitch. He dressed, filled his flask with Kahlúa and hurried outside, glancing upward, as if expecting to see the toxins in the air. By the time he reached the post office, his hands were shaking so badly he had a hard time parking his van. Finally, he left it crooked in the space and dashed into the loading area.

He picked up his new bottle of CSD, loaded his delivery bins into the mail truck in record time, and screeched out of the parking lot. *The sooner I get through this day, the better.*

While he was waiting at a traffic light, his left eye twitched rhythmically, but he did his best to ignore it. The light changed, and he drove five blocks more to the first street on his route. The sirens were still wailing. Unnerved, Eduardo opened his new bottle, squeezed three drops onto his tongue, and chased it with a swig of Kahlúa. Soon he could feel the CSD working, and his courage surged. But by the time he delivered his first load of mail, the dose seemed to have lost its potency, and he no longer felt very brave.

He went back to the truck to refill his mail satchel and took another dose for good measure. By mid-afternoon, he'd finished all the Kahlúa, and his brand-new bottle of CSD was nearly empty. Lips quivering, he closed his eyes and drained the bottle, but his courageous spirit didn't return. Despair washed over him, and he sincerely regretted using up his next week's supply of the antidote.

Eduardo gunned the engine and drove to the last neighborhood on his route. When he got out and opened the back of the truck, he noticed one of the bins had tipped over. A little white box was lying on the floor.

He picked it up to put it into his mailbag, but he couldn't make himself let go of it.

Chapter 14

10:29 AM

Tommy hunched forward in his seat as he watched the PeopleCam news broadcast that warned of lethal toxin levels for the majority of the country and listed the symptoms of chemical poisoning in the order of their progression: dizziness, disorientation, vomiting, seizures, and death. Viewers were reminded to take their doses and stay indoors if possible.

Careen stood at the window and watched black snow stain the sidewalk like ink spatters. Even from inside the house, she could taste it: metallic, tar-like. The grass in the front yard writhed and screamed as the black flakes fell upon it. *The grass can't outrun the poison, and neither can we.* The trees fought back, twisting and slapping, in a dance of futility.

A gust of wind sent the black flakes rolling like waves against the living room window. She traced the downward path of the inky rivulets with her fingertips. There was no comforting film of pink between her and the darkness of the poison snow. Only the windowpane.

Tommy got up from the sofa and stood behind her, looking out the window over her shoulder. She turned and buried her face in his chest. "What do you see?" Her voice was muffled.

"The sun is out. It's so hot the grass and leaves are wilting. That's kinda weird for November, isn't it? Why? What did you see?"

"It's snowing, but the snow is black. The sun's gone. Everything's dying."

"Right now?"

"Yes right now. How can we be seeing different things at the same time?"

He wrapped his arms around her protectively. "I dunno. Let's watch until something changes, okay?"

She turned to face the window, folded her arms over his and, clinging to him, stared through the window until she forgot what she was looking for.

4:45 PM

The sirens seemed louder than ever, and Eduardo cowered, glancing at the sky. "Just a few more blocks," he muttered. Daylight was fading, and everyone was safe inside—everyone but him. He hurried from house to house, stuffing deliveries into mailboxes with one hand while the other hand clutched the small, white box.

Halfway down the block, his eyes began to water, and his skin burned despite the chill in the air. He stopped walking and shouted, "I need it! I need it more than you, whoever you are!" There was no one around to hear his plea. He glanced at the label on the box just long enough to read the name: Thomas Bailey, Jr.

Eduardo staggered over to the curb and dropped his mailbag. He ripped open the box, dug for the bottle inside, and squeezed three drops onto his tongue. The relief that flooded over him this time was different, and stronger than ever before.

Energized, he took off at a trot. He had only a few houses left to go when he realized he actually *could* see the poison, like shards of glass floating above him, following him. But he was safe inside a force field that kept bad things at bay. *Why didn't I notice that earlier?* His eye stopped twitching.

Near the end of the block, a tunnel opened up in front of him. It glowed with a warm golden light, and the rounded walls pulsed and undulated with goodness. He scrambled inside. He smelled good things to eat, warm soup and something baking. *Bread?* All of a sudden Eduardo felt light, happy, and carefree, like a little boy. He began to skip.

5:14 PM

The mailman was very late. It was dusk when he came skipping down the middle of the street, but he made no deliveries to the houses at the end of the block.

Tommy pushed past Careen and flung open the front door. He took two steps out onto the porch but couldn't bring himself to go any farther.

"Hey! *Hey!* Where are you going? We need our doses. We're out. Come back!"

The mailman didn't seem to hear him. He staggered around the corner and out of sight.

Tommy turned back to Careen, who was peering around the doorframe. "I should've gone after him. It's Friday. What the hell? Why did he skip us?" He ducked back inside and slammed the door in frustration.

"It's Friday," Careen whispered in horror. "We won't be able to get any more antidote until Monday."

"What about yours? Where do you live?"

"We'd probably be dead long before we got to my apartment. What if being inside the house is the only thing that's protecting us? What if we chanced a trip to my apartment and my dose wasn't delivered either? I'm not going out there." She ran from room to room, looking around wildly. Finally, she scuttled under the dining room table.

He waited for her to come out, and when she failed to reappear he took a blanket off the back of the sofa and spread it over the table, then crawled partway in. She'd made a space for herself between two chairs.

"I used to make blanket forts under this table when I was little."

Tears pooled in her eyes. "A blanket fort isn't going to help. Can't you smell the poison in the air?"

"Nah." He tried to sound convincing.

"It's black snow. Real snow is clean and crisp, and this...stuff in the air is going to kill us. I dream about it all the time. I dream they set the poison off at night."

"But wouldn't that be...kind of okay? I mean, in the middle of the night you'd never know what hit you."

"So *not* okay! When all this is over and things get back to normal..."

He snorted. "Normal? How do we even know what that is?"

She brushed away a tear. "Normal should be school and work and ice cream and shopping. Normal should be someone waiting up for you when you stay out late. Normal should be complaining about the debit card bill or the loose brick on the front porch. Normal is *not* watching black snowflakes stain the sidewalk and hearing the grass scream as it's being poisoned."

He eased himself under the table as far as he could. "Normal is *not* both of us looking out the same window at the same time and seeing different things."

She fought to keep from crying. "So what can I believe?"

"Believe that I'm here—I'm real—and I'm not going anywhere. Count on it."

Chapter 15

5:45 PM
Quadrant OP-439

Eduardo wandered through the golden tunnel and found himself safely back at his mail truck. He was amazed to discover that he could balance his letter opener on the end of his nose. It was immensely entertaining to spin it like a propeller. He giggled and made airplane noises as he drove back to the post office. *Air mail. Get it?*

The traffic light was red, and he reached out through the windshield to touch it. How curious. Yesterday he'd driven this way and hadn't noticed any traffic lights at all. The lights receded into another golden tunnel, and he hit the gas to follow them.

The letter opener spun like a pinwheel in a spring breeze, until it was whirling so fast it flew off his nose. The blade plunged with surprising intensity into his thigh, and he yowled in pain. His breathing grew ragged; sweat broke out at his temples, and the van careened down the road as he struggled to pull the blade free. He didn't see the telephone pole in time to hit the brakes, and there was an almighty crash.

Horns blared all around him, and he realized he was blocking the road. He reached desperately for his flask and raised it to his lips, but it was empty.

A quadrant marshal yanked opened the driver's side door.

6:29 PM

The last remnants of daylight slipped away, and it was dark when Tommy decided he couldn't stay wedged under the dining room table one minute more. He was cramped and his butt was numb. *I wish someone could pry me out with a crowbar.*

As he pushed back a chair, Careen grabbed his arm anxiously. "Don't! It might not be safe."

"I know. But hell, if I'm going to die, I'd rather die on the sofa."

"Look outside. What do you see?"

Stiffly, he got to his feet, limped over to the front door, and flipped on the porch light. "Nothing much. It's dark. I can see the grass, though."

She hesitated, then came crawling out of their makeshift fortress. "Really? No snow?" She stood behind him and peeked around his shoulder. "I don't see it anymore! Did it melt?"

"I don't know. Let's check in with the rest of the world and see what's going on." He turned on the TV to watch the PeopleCam evening news report. Pete Sheridan looked gravely into the center camera as he read the top story.

"At least one thousand Americans were added to the martyr roll during today's nationwide chemical attack. The OCSD reports two hundred thirty-one deaths from heart attacks and five hundred forty-eight from traffic accidents caused by panic, with the remainder attributed to chemical poisoning. The death toll is expected to rise, and there may not be an accurate measure of civilian casualties for several days, until the toxin levels in the atmosphere dissipate and the OCSD teams can get an accurate count. It is imperative to keep taking your daily doses, folks."

Careen clapped her hands to her mouth and ran into the kitchen. Puzzled, Tommy followed her, but backed away when she began to vomit into the sink. He waited in the hall, willing himself to think of anything but upchucking until she was finished.

"Do you think it'd help if you ate something?" he called from a safe distance.

"Not really," she choked out. She turned on the water and rinsed her mouth.

Tommy gave her a few minutes, then joined her in the kitchen. He rummaged through the pantry and refrigerator, and soon there was a jumbled assortment of food on the counter. "I get my Essential Services delivery on Thursdays. This was supposed to last me a week, but there's a good chance I won't need it, so eat as much as you want when you feel like it." He busied himself for a minute. "Mmm… peanut butter and pickle sandwiches." He offered her one but she waved it off, covering her nose.

"That's a ridiculous last meal." She smiled in spite of herself.

"You have a better idea?"

"Given the choice, I'd have the most expensive thing on the menu at a five-star restaurant. I wouldn't even care what it was. Under the circumstances, I guess there's nothing wrong with an Essential Services smorgasbord."

They ate at the kitchen counter and decided there was no point in cleaning up. On the living room sofa, she curled up beside him and slid her toes under his leg. Tommy welcomed the friendly contact, and wished it were an ordinary day. If they'd met on any other day, this could've been their first date; maybe they'd have laughed and flirted and asked all those getting-to-know-you questions that didn't really matter anymore, even though he wished they did. That date might've ended with the thrill of a few kisses and the anticipation of more to come. *But whatever happens, I'm glad I shared my last dose with her.* They sat in silence for some time before she reached for his hand.

"I guess it's too late for us, isn't it? I'm dizzy and obviously I'm nauseated, too. How long do you think it'll take... to die?" A tear slid down her cheek, but her voice was steady.

"I dunno."

"I thought it would be over by now." She paused. "Do you think your parents will be waiting for you?"

"In someplace like heaven? I hope so." He looked down at their entwined fingers. "After the accident, it seemed like everything I had was destroyed. When I woke up in the hospital, my parents were just...gone. My leg was mangled. I had four surgeries, and still the doctors said I might never walk right again."

He pulled up the leg of his sweatpants, and she gasped at the sight of the long scar that ran up the outside of his calf, from ankle to knee, but she didn't look away. "Can I touch it?" He nodded, and she laid her hand gently on his leg. "What about now? Does it hurt?"

"Not too much. At first it did, and I let myself get depressed, and I mean *really* depressed, like I could just...give up and let myself die. But after a while, I was well enough to work out and do physical therapy, and that was when I started feeling better about everything. I figured someday I'd be okay--maybe not exactly what I was before, but still okay. Now, I'm faced with dying again, and I don't want to. Not even a little bit." He glanced sideways at her again. "What about you? Tell me about your dad. What will he do when you show up on a fluffy cloud somewhere like heaven?"

Her eyes filled with tears. "He'll say, 'whadda ya know for sure?' and I'll have to say 'I blew it, Daddy. You died trying to save me, and then I did absolutely nothing with the rest of my life.' I tried—I studied hard and got a Victory Scholarship, you know, the ones they give to kids who've lost parents to terrorist attacks. I was just getting started—and now I'm out of time. The really awful thing is, I probably wouldn't have been able to afford college at all if my dad were still alive."

"I'm sure he'd be proud of you, no matter what. And what about your mom?"

"She and I were never really close. She's kind of flighty. My dad was the glue that held our family together, and once he was gone, well, it didn't get any better. We haven't stayed in touch since I came to the university. I don't want to talk about her."

Tommy didn't know what to say. He brushed back her bangs. Her eyes were huge and moist in her pale, heart-shaped face. *So pretty. And so sad.* "Do you wanna try to rest for a while?"

"Will you wake me if…"

"If what?"

"If anything happens. If anything changes."

He felt woozy and his stomach was cramping a little, and based on that, he assumed any changes would be bad ones. He chose not to reply. Instead he retrieved the blanket from the dining-room table, spread it over them, and pulled her close.

Soon the food, exhaustion, and the comforting warmth of the shared blanket caught up with Careen, and she dozed off. Tommy, half asleep himself, pressed his lips to the top of her head and reached to switch off the light on the end table. *It's best if we don't see it coming.*

It seemed he'd only just shut his eyes when he woke to Careen's screams.

Chapter 16

2:39 AM
Day 16: Saturday, November 11, 2034
Quadrant OP-439

Tommy sat up on the sofa just in time to catch an elbow to his nose. Disoriented in the darkness, he took two more blows to his face and one to his shoulder before he had a chance to react and pin down his attacker.

He fumbled for the lamp, and when he switched it on, he found himself nose-to-nose with Careen. She was in the throes of some kind of seizure, twisting and kicking, her skin and hair damp. He was afraid to let her up, and afraid not to. Her eyes were open but glassy, and she stared through him like she was possessed or something. He went cold with dread. Seizures came right before death on the list of symptoms. If Careen was succumbing to the poison, it wouldn't be long before he did, too. He tried to provide her with what little comfort he could. "Hey, it's Tommy. I'm here. I told you I'd be here. It's gonna be okay." His gentle whispers seem to calm her. She lifted her face silently to his, and he sobbed—one gut-wrenching, solitary sound—then covered her face with salty kisses.

When Tommy drew back a little, Careen was silent and still beneath him, eyes closed, barely breathing. He traced his fingers through her hair where he imagined the pink highlights would be. He'd known her less than twenty-four hours, but that was long enough—long enough to hope that he'd no longer have to go it alone.

Tommy gently nudged her cheek with his nose, closed his eyes, and touched his lips to hers. *At least this time I'll get to say goodbye.*

Her lips parted and she kissed him back drowsily. Tommy sprang back and yelped with surprise. She opened her eyes and pushed herself to a sitting position, looking sleepy and confused. "Hey—what's the matter? Are you all right?"

He collapsed on the sofa, weak with relief. "You had some kind of seizure or something. I thought...I wasn't sure, but you were so out of it. I thought it was...over."

"Oh no!" Her eyes grew wide. "I'm so sorry if I freaked you out. It must've been night terrors. I get them when I'm stressed, but I never remember them afterward."

"Holy shit." He pulled her into a tight hug, then laughed.

"What's so funny?"

"Maybe we're not really dying after all."

"Maybe. I guess we can hope."

"Hope is good." He untangled the blanket.

"Tommy?"

"Yeah?"

"It helps to leave a light on."

"As you wish."

Chapter 17

The streets were deserted when Kevin left home and headed southwest. Once he left the suburbs around the capital, the quadrants through which he passed were sparsely populated, and he met no other cars along the way. He arrived with ten minutes to spare and was pleased that the meeting place was a diner—it was shabby, but at least it was a public place.

He trudged across the gravel parking lot, hands buried deep in his coat pockets. He glanced in through the front window before he opened the door. The place was nearly deserted and dimly lit; but he stepped in, sat at the counter, and ordered coffee. The waitress looked about fifteen—skinny and freckled, in tight jeans and a sweatshirt. She poured his coffee, then picked up a loaded tray and carried it out to the only other customers in the place. He watched her walk across the room.

"Try the pancakes."

He jumped. A huge bear of a man stood next to him, wearing a knit cap and a dark pea coat. He was easily three times Kevin's size.

"Uh, really? Okay..." he glanced around nervously.

"Yeah. They got great pancakes here." The hulking stranger called back to the cook. "Hey, Mitch! Two large stacks." Then he walked around behind the counter and poured his own cup of coffee. When he took the stool next to Kevin, their elbows touched, even though Kevin tried hard to avoid it. They nursed their coffees, and when the pancakes arrived, they both dug in.

The man beside him shoveled in huge mouthfuls. "Can't get used to the food restrictions, you know? I get over here as often as I can. Great pancakes." He bumped against Kevin with his elbow as he cut into his stack. He nodded and managed to keep his seat.

He'd cleaned his plate and was finishing his second cup of coffee when the big man stood up, clapped him on the shoulder, and walked out of the diner without saying another word.

No one else paid him the slightest attention. He glanced around and took out his debit card to pay.

The freckled waitress leaned across the counter and studied his card. "Kevin, huh?" She twirled it between her fingers and smiled, then beckoned with the card. "Come with me."

He followed her through the kitchen and out the back door, where she handed him back his debit card. "That card's no good here. We only accept barter. Anyhow, your breakfast is on Jeff today. Walk that way" –she pointed into the woods, dense with underbrush— "about a hundred yards."

He stood with his wallet in one hand and his debit card in the other, looking at her nervously.

"Go on," she shooed him onto the path. "And don't forget to say the password!"

After scrambling up and down the hilly path for what seemed like an eternity, Kevin emerged from the woods at a target range, where a dark-haired young man in jeans and a barn coat waited beside an ancient, black, four-wheel-drive pickup. The stranger held out his hand. "I'm Jeff."

"Kevin." He cleared his throat. "Uhh...*me-no see-boo err-duh?*"

"Sure."

"If it's okay to ask...what does that mean, exactly?"

"Oh, that's just a code we use that shows you've been recruited by another member. It's not too sophisticated. If you write it backwards and translate it from Latin, it means "the point of no return." But you didn't have to try to say it out loud or anything."

"The waitress said..."

Jeff rolled his eyes. "Yeah. I'm sure she did. Jaycee's quite the practical joker. In fact, she's probably still laughing at you. Come on, let's talk in the truck."

The floorboards were littered with empty diet soda cans. Kevin shuffled his feet in among them, nervously trying not to disturb anything. There were two more in the console's cup holder.

As the engine roared to life, Jeff got straight to the point. "We made contact with you because we need you to help sabotage the production of CSD."

"I don't have access to anything sensitive. I'm just a lab assistant. Who are you, anyway? Who is we?"

"We're the Resistance—a bunch of people who oppose the policies which give the OCSD the right to meddle in our lives. We work for change, using mostly what you'd call unconventional methods. Stuff they won't see coming. We want you to switch the CSD formulas on the next week's run so regular people get the placebo instead of the hard stuff and the dopes in the government offices get the dope."

"What? Are you crazy? I don't think I could do that, even if I wanted to. When all this started, I had no idea the OCSD would be telling lies and holding people prisoner and stuff. I already took a huge risk by contacting you and coming here today. They'll lock me up, too, if they even think I'm..." The very thought of it was more than he could stomach.

Jeff slammed on the brakes, flinging Kevin against the dashboard. "What do you mean, holding people prisoner?"

Kevin closed his eyes and started talking.

Chapter 18

Tommy opened his eyes, momentarily blinded by the shards of sunlight piercing the dusty airspace around him. Careen was still asleep, balled up between the cushions. He nudged her gently.

She stirred and turned over. "Mmmm."

"Hey, wake up. It's morning, and we're still alive."

She sat up, and instantly her drowsy calm changed to panic. She swallowed hard, kicked her way out of the blanket, and sprinted from the room.

He heard her heave and vomit, and that was all it took. He pounded into the kitchen and leaned over the sink.

She was lying on the sofa with her arm across her face when Tommy came back and eased himself into a chair.

"So much for that last meal," she said.

"Man, that was like the purge to end all purges. Wow."

"Yeah, but now I feel better."

"Yeah?" He thought about it for a moment. "Me, too."

"Do you notice anything different? I'm having trouble with color this morning. Unless you count the dark shadows under my eyes."

Tommy took a cautious look around the room and was baffled by what he didn't see. "Nothing's growing in here. That's weird."

"Come look." She got up and walked to the front window. "Now close your eyes," she ordered as he came up beside her. "On the count of three, open them and tell me what you see. Ready? One, two, three!"

"It's autumn!"

She nodded. "Your leaves need raking."

"Yeah!" He turned toward her, delighted. She looked pensive.

"What do you know for sure?"

"Huh?"

"Seriously, what do we know *for sure*? Let's make a list. Get a pen and paper."

He opened a drawer in the end table and handed them over. She flipped to a fresh page in the notebook. "I like writing on paper better than using a tablet. Okay, what do we know for sure? Or, I should say, what have we been led to believe?"

Tommy raised his hand like an eager student. "We have to take CSD every day to stay alive."

"Yes! I mean, wrong!"

"The toxins in the air will kill us."

"Not necessarily true." She was scribbling away.

"CSD is harmless. It's good for us."

"Again, not true. CSD made me not me."

He nodded. "I didn't want to do anything when I was taking it."

"I know, but those days are over. If everything the OCSD says is a lie and we can live without a daily dose of CSD," Careen finished writing with a flourish, "then I'm done taking it."

5:22 PM

Eduardo spent nearly twenty-four hours in a musty holding cell at the quadrant marshal station. He'd felt sick all day and had lost count of how many times he'd vomited into the steel toilet in his cell. Now he sat at a square Formica table in an interrogation room, waiting, and as he studied himself in the one-way mirror, his head and hands swelled until it seemed he was looking in a fun house mirror instead.

He giggled at his reflection as it morphed, but reined in the frivolity when one of the marshals and his post office branch supervisor entered the room and sat down across from him. The quadrant marshal spoke first.

"Eduardo Rodriguez, you stand accused of stealing a vial of CSD and of failing to deliver other vials to citizens in need on the day of an actual chemical attack. What do you have to say for yourself?"

Eduardo trembled. *I wish my flask was full.* "I needed extra doses to do my job. I was out in that poison all day. How else can I protect myself so I can fight the terrorists?"

The post office supervisor's stern glare pinned Eduardo to his chair like a bug stuck to corkboard in a high school science project. "How many boxes of CSD did you fail to deliver?"

He considered this. "I don't know. After I went into the tunnel, I guess I missed some houses."

"Obviously you're not up to the responsibility of serving the people on your appointed rounds. I'm sorry, but you're terminated from your employment with the US Postal Service, effective immediately."

The quadrant marshal stood and took Eduardo by the arm. "I need to know exactly which houses you skipped. If any of those people died, you may be charged with manslaughter."

"I didn't mean to hurt anyone. I want to help my country. What can I do to make it right?"

The marshal shrugged. "That remains to be seen."

5:45 PM

Wes Carraway pulled into the parking lot at work, and right away a frantic Henry Nelson ran toward his truck.

"Man, where have you been? They've been trying to reach you for hours. I covered for you, but it's been crazy here! We had a bunch of missed deliveries yesterday afternoon."

Carraway feigned surprise. He'd received the messages, but he couldn't exactly tell them he'd be late because he was at a clandestine meeting on behalf of the Resistance. "I guess my phone battery was dead. What happened? Is everyone okay?" He made a show of plugging his phone into the charging port on his console.

"Some postman had a bad reaction to his new dose, went completely loopy and missed a bunch of houses. People started calling the hotline Friday after close of business when they realized they didn't get their mail, and they sent us out with replacement bottles for everyone. Now the postman's back down to earth, and he's given us a list of the houses he thinks he missed. They've all called in but one, so I'm on my way over there." He recited the address.

Shit. That's Bailey's address. Wes shrugged nonchalantly. "I'll go. Least I can do, since you had my back today. "

"Hey, thanks! You want me to ride along?"

"Nah. I'll call if I need backup."

Wes drove across town, his mind whirling. After speaking with Kevin, he'd realized he'd been pushing Careen toward Tom Bailey, Jr., while Mitch was seeking Tom Bailey, Sr. But maybe the kid knew his father's secret. *Mitch never takes his dose, and when I saw him today he was fine. Odds are Tommy is fine, too. By now he's probably realized he doesn't need CSD. Maybe he can help the Resistance.* He sped up.

He parked down the block, strode up to the front porch and glanced in the window. *Holy crap.* Tommy Bailey was seated at the dining-room table, eating dinner with Careen Catecher. They were interacting normally—talking, making eye contact with each other. She smiled at something he said, and Wes felt a stab of envy. Tommy was having a perfectly pleasant evening. With her.

Just then his phone beeped; Wes quickly punched the mute button and tiptoed off the porch. He stood in the shadow of the shrubbery, opened the message and swore under his breath. *Duty calls, and it has rotten timing.* He ran back to his car. Now that Careen had made contact with Tommy, he needed to watch them even more closely.

Chapter 19

Tommy and Careen continued to experience nausea throughout the day; after each purge, they ate hungrily.

Coverage of the attack and its aftermath was mandatory programming, and PeopleCam reported dangerous toxins lingering in the air nationwide. Defiantly, Careen ventured out to the backyard and stood under the patio arbor, breathing deep, daring the news reports to be true; but she experienced no new symptoms. She hugged herself in the chilly air and was struck by a sudden thought: was it too late to study for finals? Now that she wasn't taking CSD, she'd have a huge advantage over everyone who was lying around doing nothing. She wondered if she and Tommy were the only ones who'd figured it out. Had anyone else stopped taking his or her doses?

After dinner she felt restless, and impatient to get back to work. She soon lost interest in the movie Tommy was watching and wandered through the house, stopping in what must've been his father's office. Floor-to-ceiling bookshelves covered two walls, and she perused the titles: political science, history, economics, law. *I don't know anyone who has this many print books. I can study right here!* She took one off the shelf and soon was so engrossed she didn't notice when Tommy came up behind her. He put his hands on her shoulders and slid them down to her waist, but she pulled away from his touch.

"What's the matter?"

"Nothing. I'd just rather you weren't so…familiar."

"How's that?"

"I mean it. I hardly know you." She clutched the book to her chest like a suit of armor for her heart.

"You showed up here yesterday uninvited, freaked out when you thought we were gonna die, and woke me up screaming in the middle of the night. I've spent more time talking to you than anyone else in, like, the last three months, but now you hardly know me and don't want us to be familiar?"

"Oh come on! I couldn't help the way I acted or anything that happened yesterday. It was the CSD! In my dream you were really important to me, and I thought if I came here I might get some…answers." She involuntarily gripped her left forearm.

There was no nonchalance in his eyes, only hope. "And what's the verdict?"

"I don't have any answers, and apparently you don't either."

He lifted his chin, and it shifted the angle of his gaze. Just like that, he had retreated, wary. "I dreamed about you, too, you know." It sounded like a challenge.

"You did? When?"

"Two nights ago." He gestured into the space between them. "I thought maybe our dreams meant we had some kind of connection."

"Like déjà vu? I don't believe in that stuff." She knew what she had to say next would hurt him. She yanked up her sleeve and held out her forearm so he could see the writing. "Look. This is the real reason I came here. I don't know who wrote it or what it means, and now I realize you can't help me. I'm not interested in any other kind of connection with you, or anyone, right now. I'd rather be on my own."

He seemed surprised to see his address written on her arm, but as she spoke, his eyes narrowed enough to sever any perceived connection between them. "Fine. It's not that big a deal. Don't let the door hit you on the way out." He thundered down the hall, leaving Careen to stew in the silence that remained. When she came timidly into the living room, Tommy flung himself on the sofa and stared at the TV, refusing to meet her eyes.

7:55 PM

"You wanted to see me, sir?" Wes stepped into his commander's office. The commander looked up at him and frowned.

"I've discovered some disturbing things about you, Carraway."

Wes held his breath and waited, inwardly cringing. He'd only been assigned to OP-439 a short time ago, but the list of his transgressions was long: he'd stolen information from a confidential file about a suspected terrorist, he'd repeatedly broken into the home of the subject of that confidential file, and he'd arrested an innocent man. Even worse, had his commander learned he was working with the Resistance? Wes imagined he'd find all of it disturbing.

"Your personnel file got here a mere two weeks after your transfer, which, first of all, has to be some kind of land speed record. But that file tells me you've failed to complete your requisite hours of recertification, and you've not been properly instructed in the disaster protocol for this quadrant. We have more resources here in the land of the rich and privileged, and you need to get up to speed, Carraway. If I read things right, the only equipment at your last post was a flashlight, an axe, and an armband for each marshal. Probably had tin air-raid helmets and a hand-crank siren too, am I right? They trained you to function in the Dark Ages, son, and now you're gonna be pulling extra shifts to read our equipment and protocols until you're ready to join us in the current century. In case you didn't notice, we're right smack in the middle of a disaster and you need to know what to do. But that doesn't mean I'm taking you off patrols. You're young. You can go without sleep for a week or two."

"Yes sir." Wes tried not to react, either to his relief or his dismay.

"Now go get that mailman out of his holding cell and get him out of here. He totaled his postal truck yesterday, and I don't want him causing any more trouble on his way home."

8:27 PM

Eduardo followed Carraway to a waiting vehicle and slid, trembling with fear and fatigue, onto the sticky gray vinyl of the passenger seat.

"So you say you wanna do something to help, huh?" Carraway started the car. "That's great, considering how much you screwed up yesterday."

Eduardo's left eyelid was twitching again. They drove in silence, and soon they were back in the neighborhood where he delivered the mail. *Used to deliver the mail.*

"If you really wanna help, I'll set you up in a stakeout to watch what goes on in that white house on the corner." He handed Eduardo a business card. "Call me, and only me, if anything happens, if anyone comes by. I'll move your personal vehicle to an inconspicuous spot nearby and bring you some sandwiches and coffee in a couple hours."

Carraway pulled the car over to the curb and stopped, then handed him a black fleece jacket and a pair of gloves. "It's supposed to be cold tonight. You might need these." Eduardo got out of the car and pulled on the jacket gratefully.

"And here." Carraway produced a little white box. "It's the special blend reserved for marshals and military personnel. I got you switched over. Should help."

Eduardo snatched the box before he could change his mind, clutching it close to his chest with a surge of relief.

As Carraway drove off, Eduardo took a dose and pocketed his bottle. He recognized the house on the corner, and hoped Tommy was all right. He certainly hadn't meant to hurt him. He'd always liked that kid. Eduardo moved cautiously across the front lawn and slipped between the dense, bristly hedges. He stood on tiptoe to peek in the living room window and watched as Tommy marched into the room, followed by a dark-haired girl he'd never seen before. He was soon caught up in the drama of their body language, wondering what was going on; when they moved away from the window, he craned to see where they'd gone. Then the front door opened without warning, and he ducked into the shrubbery.

9:09 PM

Tommy clenched his fist around the remote and resisted the urge to throw it against the wall. He was too hurt by Careen's rejection to care about anything else at the moment. If she wanted to leave, so be it. He wasn't about to try to stop her. But Careen just stood in the open doorway, unmoving, with both hands on the screen door. When she turned to face him, her shoulders sagged and she bowed her head. Assuming an apology was forthcoming, he sat up and waited for her to speak.

"I can't go out there. It's too dark. Dark is…it's like my kryptonite, okay?"

Tommy raised an eyebrow. "You're kidding, right?"

"No. I guess the CSD kinda blurred everything. I forgot how it feels to be afraid."

"So you want me to walk you home? Check under the bed and in the closet? Keep the boogeyman away? Not likely." Then he noticed a nearly imperceptible tremor that seemed to ripple in silent waves down her body. He sighed. "Oh, hell, you can sleep on the sofa and I'll walk you home in the morning."

"I'll be fine by myself."

"Yeah, I can see that. You've got it all under control." He tossed the remote on the coffee table and limped up the stairs.

Alone, Careen locked the front door, slipped off her boots, and lay on the sofa, wrapping herself in the cozy blanket she'd shared with Tommy the night before. She'd wanted to leave, but the blanket was still more comforting than anything that awaited her at home. She wondered if it was a mistake to push him away.

She rolled over and tugged at the blanket, trying hard not to think about kissing him. *Of course I feel a connection. We thought we were going to die, and so we have a bond of sorts.* And there was definitely something about him, even if it was a fragile kind of something. She was used to hiding her heart, but Tommy wanted, needed, someone to care about. She couldn't bear to cause him more hurt than she already had.

Her face grew hot as she thought about her only other relationship experience, which had been strange and one-dimensional. Those hookups were nothing more than a response to the effects of CSD, and though the details were pretty hazy, what she recalled more than anything about those liaisons was a sense of power. That power—*her* power—was intoxicating, and although she was embarrassed to admit it, she'd eagerly taken extra doses to heighten the intensity of the ride. But she'd felt no emotional connection whatsoever. She felt far closer to Tommy, reluctant as she was to trust her own judgment. *Any feelings I think I have for Tommy are because of some meaningless dream and the fear of imminent death. He deserves someone who's ready to love him back. He deserves someone better than broken me.* She buried her face in the pillow. *I don't want to be the one he needs.*

Chapter 20

Careen was waiting at the dining-room table when Tommy came downstairs. He leaned against the doorframe, arms folded, a look of stark disinterest on his face.

"Tommy, I want to apologize." She dropped her gaze and stared into her coffee mug. "You're a really nice guy, and I was awful to you yesterday. I appreciate the way you shared your CSD with me and tried to save my life even though you hardly knew me, and I'm truly sorry for the way I treated you." She looked up at him sorrowfully.

"Told you. It's no big deal." His expression didn't waver.

"Yes, it is. It's a big deal to me. Everything that happened over the last two days was just so overwhelming." A crooked half-smile was all she could muster. "Let's go out and I'll buy you breakfast. I think I ate too much of your food yesterday."

It was an extravagant gesture, to spend money on extra food, and Tommy's expression softened as he nodded. He lent her a jacket, and they sipped coffee as they walked. Crowds of people thronged the sidewalks in the shopping district, pushing their way into the stores. Careen stopped to stare at the front of one trendy boutique.

"Look at all the people lined up outside that store—and it's not even open! Come on! I want to do an experiment." She pulled him through the crowd, dug in her bag, and fished out a key. As she opened the door and stepped inside, people spilled in around her, grabbing clothing off the racks, shoving their way through the store without even stopping to look at what they'd selected.

She looked back at him and he shrugged, holding his coffee mug out of the way as he was jostled by a woman loaded down with an armful of sweaters and a winter coat. Careen stepped behind the counter and hurriedly swiped debit cards and bagged purchases.

Tommy joined her, and in less than an hour the crowd had cleared, along with most of the merchandise. He stepped over the few remaining sweaters and a pair of jeans that lay trampled on the floor, and turned the key in the lock.

"Unbelievable."

"I'll say." She pointed over his shoulder. A new crowd was forming, pressing at the shop window.

He shook his head emphatically. "Not doing that again. Does this place have a back door? You still owe me breakfast."

She smiled as they slipped through the stock room and out into the alley. They headed down the street toward the bakery, fighting against a current of determined shoppers. One man staggered past with several rolls of upholstery fabric, and a woman with a coiled hose slung over her shoulder and a shopping bag full of garden gnomes on her arm knocked Tommy off balance as she hurried by.

There was a long line outside the jewelry store, and the bakery was full of customers. Careen's whispers were barely audible above the buzz of the hungry crowd. "What's going on? Where did all these people come from?"

He had no answer. They waited their turn in line, chose some pastries from what was left in the display case, and had their coffee mugs refilled. Careen paid with her debit card, and they slipped out of the shop. As they walked, she noticed the corner news ticker's message. "HOLIDAY SHOPPERS SEEK BARGAINS! FOURTH-QUARTER RETAIL SPENDING PROJECTED TO BE UP 500%."

"That isn't normal either, is it?" Tommy shook his head wonderingly as they continued on.

They found a vacant park bench and ate from the bakery box. As they watched the crowd go by, she whispered, "They're all buying things they couldn't possibly need. I don't understand what's going on."

"It's like they can't stop themselves," he agreed. "Can anyone afford to buy expensive stuff these days?"

"Around here, yes, I bet they can. But what if it's like this all over, in places where people don't have a lot of extra money? Yesterday I was mad about how CSD had messed up my life. But Tommy, what if we're the only ones who can think for ourselves? Look at them!"

The crowd was getting larger.

"I know what I said last night about leaving, but I think we should stick together until we can figure out what's going on. Is it okay if I stay with you a while longer?"

He bumped his shoulder playfully against hers and took a sip of coffee. "Count on it."

12:40 PM

"I looked in the window and saw Tommy arguing with the pretty girl. She acted like she was going to leave, but I guess she changed her mind. They must've made up because they went out to breakfast and shopping together this morning." Eduardo leaned in the driver's-side window and breathlessly gave his report to Wes Carraway.

"What stores did they go to?"

Eduardo told him.

"Keep on it." Wes kept a stern face, but he was pleased at Eduardo's dedication to the task. He was trustworthy and willing. With Eduardo keeping watch over Tommy and Careen, he'd be able to get a few hours' sleep every now and then.

Chapter 21

8:35 AM
Day 18: Monday, November 13, 2034
Quadrant DC-001

Trina followed Dr. Stratford and Madalyn into the secure ward. Stratford swiped his ID through the reader and accessed a dimly-lit room where a pale, sickly-looking man lay buckled into his hospital bed beneath the blankets and restraints. The cloying scent of stale, sour sweat permeated the tiny room. Wire-rimmed glasses lay on the metal bedside table.

Dr. Stratford made a few notes on his tablet and then handed it to Trina. *Subject A remains most uncooperative. Subject B has experienced normal withdrawal symptoms at the anticipated intervals. Extending time between Subject B's doses of Phase Two by one hour to encourage Subject A's full cooperation, but must re-dose Subject B before detoxification symptoms wane.*

He leaned in close and spoke to the man. "I'm going to let your wife go an extra hour before her dose today. Maybe that will help you remember the answers to my questions."

Stratford stalked out of the room, but Trina waited as Madalyn lingered in the doorway, looking back at the man, who moaned and thrashed weakly against his restraints. Down the hall, they looked in on a woman with a mass of curly red hair that gleamed in the shadows. She tossed and turned in her sleep as if struggling to escape the grip of some unseen demon. Stratford paused briefly in front of another door, and then entered a room at the end of the hall. The martyr, Sid Friedman, lay snoring in his bed. Trina stared ahead, eyes unfocused, until Madalyn demanded her attention.

"Go get us coffee and bring it to Dr. Stratford's office."

Trina left the room obediently. But once out of sight, she paused to make sure the ward's security door was unlocked.

9:20 AM

Kevin glanced around to make sure the coast was clear before slipping stealthily through the unlocked door into the secure ward. He tiptoed down the hall, a cautious glance into each observation window providing the answer he needed. Five. There were five people being held here. He worked his way back down the hall, trying each door. The first four were locked, but on the last try he got lucky. Kevin opened the door just enough to see inside. The man in the bed called out desperately, "Lara!"

I wish I could help him—help them all—but I need backup. He closed the door and let himself out of the ward as quietly as he could, but the security door closed with a resounding click that seemed to echo in the empty hall. He heard footsteps, and ducked around the corner out of sight. The hiss of the security door confirmed what he suspected: he'd just dodged a deadly bullet.

Chapter 22

"Carraway, did you really forget to take a bottle of antidote with you when you checked out the situation at the Bailey home on Saturday afternoon?"

Shit shit shit. "Well, sir, it didn't seem necessary to leave a bottle of the antidote. The individual still had enough left to last through the weekend, and he said he'd call the hotline today."

The captain frowned. "Son, I know you've been burning the candle at both ends, but this is just sloppy work. Go find Nelson and get over there pronto. When you get back, he's going to verify that you gave that kid his antidote, then you can write up the report. That's an order."

"Yes sir."

9:15 AM

Tommy left the house later than usual. He swung into an old, familiar five-mile loop through his neighborhood and maintained a good pace as he ran. *Three days without any CSD, and I feel like my old self again.* He saw people out walking on every street, but no one seemed to notice him. They all moved briskly in the same direction. *It's like they're in a movie and I'm the spectator.*

When he jogged around the last corner, he noticed an unfamiliar black car parked in front of his house. As he approached, four people stepped out to meet him.

Beth Severson waved to him. Her husband, Art, was with her, but Tommy didn't recognize the other two men. He slowed to a walk.

"Tommy, honey, we've been worried about you. We knocked and you didn't answer the door. Are you okay?" As Beth approached him, he took an involuntary step back. She'd been the next best thing to a mom, and he'd trusted her, loved her a little, even. Now her look was vacant, and though she was saying all the right things, something was definitely wrong. She reminded him of the way Careen had looked during her episode of night terrors.

Art Severson stepped up beside his wife. "Did you know some people on your street didn't get their Friday deliveries? Everyone called the distribution hotline number but you. We were afraid something bad had happened. You okay, buddy?"

"He looks fine, doesn't he? Look at him, Art. He looks just fine. Did you take your dose this morning?" Beth laid a maternal hand on Tommy's forehead, like he might have a fever.

"Uh…yeah. Yeah. I got my delivery. No worries."

"But you haven't taken it yet, have you?" The two men he didn't know suddenly stepped forward, and Tommy found himself surrounded, trapped on his own front lawn.

"Why? What's going on?"

"When there's any question, any problem with deliveries in a quadrant, we're required to follow up. It's our job to watch you take your next dose and make sure there are no ill effects." He flashed his badge. "Wes Carraway. Quadrant Marshals."

Tommy sized up the two marshals. Carraway was practically a kid, only a few years older than he was. And he looked fit. Really fit. *I don't have much chance of overpowering them both. Or outrunning them.*

He scrubbed at his hair and feigned indifference, then brushed past Beth and sauntered toward the front porch. "Yeah, okay. Whatever. I'll go inside and take it." He had his hand on the doorknob when Carraway stepped up and blocked his way.

"We need to *see* you take it. Right now."

The second marshal twisted Tommy's arm behind his back and held his head. Carraway produced a bottle and dropper and deftly squeezed three drops into Tommy's mouth. He jerked his head free, hoping at least a drop of the CSD would be lost in the sweat and spit that sprayed across the front of Carraway's jacket.

Carraway pulled him up by his sweatshirt and whispered urgently. "I know she's here. What have you told her?"

"Huh? Who? I don't know…" They looked at each other, nose to nose, for a long, agonizing moment, before Carraway released him and dropped the bottle into the pocket of his sweatshirt. The two marshals strode away, and Tommy slumped against the door. *That dose was wicked strong.* He fumbled with the doorknob, desperate to get inside. He was losing control, fast.

Beth Severson smiled and waved as she herded her husband into the back seat of the car. "Bye, sweetie! Glad you're okay."

Careen was waiting in the front hall when he staggered into the house. She turned the deadbolt as he slid listlessly down the wall and made no effort to hide her tears as she knelt beside him.

"Oh my God, Tommy! I'm so sorry. I heard the whole thing. They knocked earlier, while you were gone, but I was afraid to open the door. I should've tried to help you."

"Would've dosed you, too." He tried to focus on her face, but it was a losing battle. "They know someone's here with me, so be careful. Stay hidden. And listen—this dose is different. Stronger." He gripped her arm and tried to blink away the blinding snow that swirled around the edges of his vision. As it closed over him he whispered, "Watch me."

Careen caught Tommy's head as he lost consciousness, and eased him down to the floor. She slipped a pillow from the sofa under his head and used their favorite blanket to cover him where he lay on the rug in the front hall, then settled into a living room chair where she could keep a watchful eye on him and still have the television for company. The news reports focused on the growing lists of casualties, which Careen assumed were fabrications. The news was sure to be devoid of anything truthful.

Around noon, Tommy grew restless and cried out in his drug-induced stupor. He shuddered and his teeth chattered. Careen couldn't wake him, so she knelt beside him and tried to calm him, stroking his hair and murmuring in what she hoped was a comforting way. When he finally grew quiet, she tiptoed back to the living room and dozed off in the chair, never noticing a new message that flashed across the screen: REPORT FOR TRAINING 19:00.

At dusk Tommy woke with a start, threw off the blanket, and strode into the kitchen without a word. When she heard him rummaging around, she peeked around the corner and watched as he wolfed down a hastily-made sandwich. He wiped his mouth with the back of his hand and walked past her up the stairs as if he didn't see her standing there.

When he came back down twenty minutes later, he was dressed in black track pants and a wrinkled, gray sweatshirt, a duffel bag slung over his shoulder. She met him at the bottom step and blocked his way. "Whatcha doing?"

"I gotta go." There was no inflection in his voice.

"Where?" She grabbed his arm, but he threw off her grasp and headed toward the door. She stepped in front of him again, more urgently. "Tommy, you have to stay here with me, remember?" She reached up and took his face in both hands, but he didn't meet her gaze. There was something dangerous about him, like a kind of energy, pulsing beneath his skin.

He brushed her hands away as though she were a bothersome insect and shouldered past her. "I gotta go." He stepped out into the night. Horrified, she watched him stride across the lawn. She hesitated until he was almost out of sight, then dashed after him.

Chapter 23

9:20 AM
Quadrant DC-001

"Davies, Jacobs, we've got a lot of work to do before the press conference on Thursday. We'll be celebrating the success of the CSD program. First the president will announce to the public that soon they'll be safe, as the terrorist threat is nearly eradicated. Then I'll have a ceremonial dose of CSD with the president and the chief quadrant marshal. I'll need you girls to handle the details and coordinate the live broadcast with PeopleCam."

Trina near lost it. *I'm not even close to cracking the sequence codes.* Production would begin that night on the next week's supply of CSD, so it could be distributed Friday. Each production code sequence was over two hundred characters long, and she had no idea what to alter. She needed a faster, less technical way to counteract Stratford's plan. But what?

6:09 PM

By the end of the day, Trina was frazzled from alternating between working on the details of the press conference with Madalyn and her own clandestine efforts to make sense of the sequence codes, but she managed to maintain her outward mask of CSD-induced calm. Now she'd been summoned to Lowell Stratford's office, and sat with her hands folded in her lap as he showed her three identical amber bottles in a white velvet-lined presentation case.

"I prepared these doses of CSD myself. Do you like the case? I ordered it before the launch of Phase One. It's for the press conference. See? There's one for the president, one for the chief quadrant marshal, and one for me."

He's talking to me like I'm a dim-witted five-year-old.

"Trina, I have a great deal of respect for you as a doctor, but you opposed me in front of our colleagues, and I couldn't let you undermine my plan. Actually, I'm surprised how much I like you now. You're so much easier to deal with, and I feel like I can talk to you."

If you only knew how I feel about you, you power-tripping lunatic.

"When I became head of the OCSD, I believed the American people would understand that my sole objective was to keep them safe from harm. I worked tirelessly, and I was confident that people would appreciate my efforts and follow me willingly.

"The OCSD director's post is…well, it's like an end-run around the process other people go through to become a world leader, like a president. Everyone turns to me to make the truly important decisions. The president listens to everything I say, and Congress agrees to everything I propose.

"It's regular people like you, Trina, who are the problem. Some of you just don't know how to follow. In fact, the ones who resist me most are the ones who need to be led, because for some reason they can't see that I'm right.

"My goal is to crush the foreign invaders who threaten our great nation—and that's nothing new. It's a goal shared by every generation of leaders since ancient times. I have the power, the means, and the technology to do things those ancient warriors never dreamed of, but I can't have anyone standing in my way or questioning me. Soon, everyone will be on Phase Three, and I'll be in control. No more placebos.

"I'm a great leader. I can resolve any conflict. I can provide safety, security, and jobs. I can take away stress. It's all possible with CSD because people will actually follow my lead. I've integrated man and hallucination for the betterment of society, and soon everyone will take their place in the final phase of my great plan."

Stratford smiled as he locked the white velvet presentation case in his desk drawer.

Not if my plan works first. Trina bowed her head, fighting the rush of hatred and eagerness for battle that threatened to give her away.

Chapter 24

6:51 PM
Quadrant OP-439

Tommy walked down the street with purpose, his sun-bleached hair glowing in the light from the street lamps.

Careen skirted the pools of lamplight as she ran after him. Fallen leaves crunched under her feet and skittered on the breeze. She was terrified of the darkness, but she was even more afraid of being too visible.

He turned a corner, and as she hurried to catch up, she was startled to see throngs of men and women walking in the same direction, all dressed in dark clothing. She lost track of Tommy in the growing crowd, and before she could be swept along against her will, she slipped into the shadow of a massive oak tree and scanned the faces of the people who passed. No one spoke. Their feet moved in unison, as though they all heard the same distant drumbeat.

Tommy had to be far ahead of her by now. She screwed up her courage and was just about to leave her hiding place and continue searching when she heard another set of footsteps moving in a different, frantic rhythm.

A young man ran against the flow of the crowd, shoving people out of his way as he tried to elude the two quadrant marshals who pursued him. At the corner, the marshals overtook him and grabbed him roughly by the arms. As they struggled, she shrank farther into the shadows. Several more people marched by, but no one spared a glance for the young man or tried to help him.

The marshals beat him with their nightsticks until he fell to the pavement, then kicked him repeatedly. She turned away and covered her ears to muffle the thump of steel-toed boots on flesh and the young man's groans.

The marshals dragged the still, bloody figure out of the light, dumped him in the shadows just a few yards from where she was hiding, and swaggered away to patrol the crowd.

I didn't help him. I didn't do anything to stop it. Careen's heart was pounding. *But how could I? I'm only one person. I can't stop any of this.*

She strained to see in the darkness. The young man's arm covered his face, but she saw fair hair gleaming faintly in the glow of the street lamp. *What if that's Tommy?* Panic overtook her, and she crawled out of the tree's protective embrace. She stopped a few feet from the broken body, listening, watching, for any sign of life. Then she heard him take a gurgling breath. She swallowed hard, pushing back her fear, and tugged at his sleeve until his arm moved and she could see his face. It wasn't Tommy.

The stranger's gaze met Careen's and he clutched at her arm as he struggled to speak. His words came out a raspy whisper. "Death is not the worst of evils." A bloody bubble formed and burst on his lips, and then he was still. She watched the light fade from his eyes. *Oh God, not again.*

Her father had tried to downplay his injuries as he lay pinned in the rubble after the bomb blast. She had been too small and weak to free him, and too frightened to find a way out of the shattered building. She told herself that had she known he was critically wounded, she would have found a way to save him. *Don't worry,* he'd said. *Someone will be here soon. Sing me a song. Tell me about what you're learning in school.* When it grew dark, he grew quiet. She'd spent that night waiting beside her father's body, and woke the next morning to realize he was dead, his lifeless, open eyes still watching over her.

Now, alone in the dark with another dead man, Careen covered her face with her hands and rocked back and forth on her knees. His eyes were open, but he did not see her mourn or hear her anguished, grief-stricken sobs. The sound of an approaching vehicle startled Careen from her lamentation, and she ran into the deep shadows of a nearby house.

Headlights cut across the lawn. The two marshals jumped out of a Jeep, loaded the body in the back, and sped away.

For tonight, anyway, the darkness is my ally. She started toward Tommy's house, slipping through the gloom as quickly and quietly as she could. Twice more she had to duck and cover, using shrubbery to camouflage herself as Jeeps roared past. The unexpected detours left her disoriented, and she wasn't sure how to get back. She hugged herself against the cold and her rising panic and forced herself to think calmly. Most houses were dark this late at night, but she'd run out in a hurry and left all the downstairs lights on.

She crept out into the street and turned in a circle, looking for a well-lit house. *There! That house one street over has an arbor on the patio, and all the lights are on.* In her relief, she moved recklessly through the backyards, disturbing fallen leaves and setting some shrubs rustling.

She was halfway up the path beside the garage when a man stepped out of the shadows and pressed his nose against the kitchen window. She froze in her tracks and glanced around for a weapon, then picked up a rock about the size of a baseball from the flowerbed. A broom leaned against the garage. She took a deep breath and put her plan into action.

8:31 PM

Eduardo watched the house all day, but he'd noticed nothing since Carraway dosed Tommy early that morning. Just before dark, he'd run out of Kahlúa and made a trip to the liquor store to buy more. Upon his return, he'd picked his way carefully through the overgrown bushes, looking in the ground-floor windows, but saw no one.

He was on tiptoe, attempting to see in the kitchen window, when he heard a crash at the corner of the house. Startled, he ran away from the noise into the deep shadows of the backyard. He didn't see what hit him, but he fell flat on his back, stunned. When he finally regained his senses, he noticed that the blinds were closed in the downstairs windows.

8:33 PM

Careen sat on the floor beneath the bank of kitchen windows that looked out over the back yard, broom across her knees, breathing hard.

Well, that didn't go the way I thought it would!

As her adrenaline rush subsided, Careen began to giggle. She'd thrown the rock at the trashcans, assuming the man would investigate the noise and enable her to make a run for the front door around the other side of the house. Instead, he'd run away from the noise and right into her path. She didn't have time to veer, so she instinctively swung the broom handle and caught him under the chin. He went down hard, and she used his misfortune to her advantage: she sprinted for the house, locked herself in, and hurried from room to room, shutting drapes and closing blinds.

When she'd dared to peek out the kitchen window, she'd seen the man get shakily to his feet and stagger out of the yard. Now that she was alone, she was overcome by uncontrollable laughter. It had been an awful night. She felt guilty that she'd given up on her search for Tommy. She'd witnessed a murder. She'd attacked someone for the first time in her life. And none of it was remotely funny. Her laughter turned to sobs.

Half an hour later, she hauled herself up, spent but calm; she settled in for her third night on Tommy's sofa, and waited for him to come home.

Chapter 25

6:51 AM
Day 19: Tuesday, November 14, 2034
Quadrant OP-439

Careen lay awake, listening. When she heard footsteps on the porch steps and the click of a key in the lock, she ran into the front hall, security blanket in tow. She threw her arms around Tommy as he stepped inside, and though he staggered a bit at the moment of impact, he managed to stay on his feet. She clung to him, hoping the embrace would adequately convey a few things she couldn't seem to say out loud, and after a few seconds his arms went around her, too. She almost sobbed with relief, but then his arms slipped listlessly down to his sides. She took a step back and gasped at what she saw. His eyes were half closed with fatigue. His lip was swollen, and he had a nasty cut over his left eyebrow and the beginnings of a black eye. His forearms were bruised and he was flecked with mud and blood.

"Where have you been?" she asked gently.

He rubbed his good eye and answered, "Football practice," then slowly climbed the stairs, stepping on each tread with both feet before moving up to the next one. Soon she heard him start the shower.

The disaster sirens keened and the female voice proclaimed that this was not a drill. *Yeah, yeah.* Careen rolled her eyes.

After a few minutes she went upstairs, peeked in his bedroom, and found him fast asleep on top of his rumpled covers, mouth slightly open, one arm thrown out to the side. In his relaxed state, she could see what he must've looked like as a little boy. She felt a surge of tenderness for him, and a desire to be close to him, even if he didn't know she was there. She opened the closet door and found an extra quilt, spread it over him, and crawled in wearily. She pressed close to his side and drifted off, breathing in the scents of soap and his warm skin.

His eyes were still closed, but Tommy was awake, mentally attempting to inventory his aches and pains. There were so many that he wondered if he'd played football without pads. His ribs must be bruised; it hurt to breathe deeply. Hell, everything hurt. He resolved to lay there as long as possible, but then his stomach cramped so violently that he groaned aloud and drew his knees to his chest. He tried to twist away from the pain, but there was no place to escape. The quilt ensnared him, and he rolled off the bed and landed hard, the jolt of his crash-landing momentarily distracting him from the agonizing ache in his gut. Careen's face appeared over the edge of the bed. She said something, but it felt as if a huge hand was squeezing his insides, and his head was pounding so loudly he couldn't hear her. The black snow was back, clouding his vision. *This is not a drill. Shit.* His body craved what was in the amber bottle, and he found it where that quadrant marshal had left it—in the pocket of the sweatshirt he'd worn yesterday.

His hands shook as he unscrewed the lid. *Three drops.* In seconds, the pain receded.

Tommy heard Careen shouting, but she was so far away he couldn't understand her. She knelt on his bed as it floated on the lake that sparkled in the blinding sunlight.

This time when Tommy hit the floor he didn't feel a thing.

Careen had been sleeping soundly, and, bleary-eyed, she reacted too slowly. She didn't have time to do more than cry out in frustration as she watched Tommy squeeze a dose from the dropper and collapse on the floor.

She shook her head. *Fool me once, shame on you. Fool me twice...* She picked up the bottle and looked around for a suitable hiding place, choosing to stash it in the closet, way back on the top shelf. Then she did what she could to make him comfortable on the floor. *Déjà vu all over again,* she thought grimly. His peaceful, childlike sleep was over, and he twitched and grimaced. As she tiptoed out of the room, she heard him mutter, "I'll rip your head off." She glanced back, making sure he was still in the grip of the antidote. He sounded savage, almost inhuman, and for the first time she was afraid of him.

Careen spent part of the afternoon foraging for useful things. She found a flashlight in the kitchen junk drawer, and when she put it in her messenger bag she found her phone. She turned it on and discovered two new government-issued messages. One was from Sunday morning. It read GO SHOPPING. The other was from Monday afternoon: REPORT FOR TRAINING 19:00.

A chill rippled through her body. She thought about all the people she'd seen over the past two days who had seemed compelled to act in a certain way, to do things they wouldn't normally do. *Why would they blindly obey these messages?*

She checked Tommy's messages on the television, and they were the same as hers. Neither of them had had the urge to shop, but there was no way she could've kept Tommy from going out last night after he was dosed. This round of CSD had to be different somehow, just like he'd said. She resolved to be ready to follow him the next time he went out and not let him slip away.

She searched for some suitable clothing in what had been his parents' room, and found some dark wool pants and a heavy black sweater in his mother's closet that fit well enough and would camouflage her in the shadows. She showered and changed, by now accustomed to the sirens that wailed off and on throughout the day. Conscious of their dwindling food supply, she waited as long as possible before rooting through what was left in the pantry and the fridge and preparing a simple meal.

The top news story on PeopleCam announced a local casualty in the day's chemical attack. *I haven't had any symptoms. How can someone here be dead from the poison?* More dubious than curious, she sat down to watch.

When the martyr died, PeopleCam had devoted a week to his death, his funeral, his legacy. Since then, PeopleCam had singled out and profiled a few people reported killed since Distribution Day, but this story was different. Pete Sheridan was not his usual jovial self. He seemed distracted, and missed his cue. His eyes were red-rimmed, and his chin trembled for a moment before he began to read from the teleprompter. "Now, I ask you viewers at home, haven't we all had enough time to establish good habits? Haven't we been instructed and reminded to take our CSD? How foolish—how wasteful—that this young man from a good family, with everything going for him, could not do what he was told and protect himself.

"This once-promising member of society succumbed to the effects of the poison around noon today. His family will hold a private memorial service later this week in an undisclosed location."

He furrowed his brow and pounded his fist on the news desk. "And let this be a lesson to anyone out there who thinks they don't have to follow the rules. Don't end up dead like this irresponsible boy."

Careen gasped as the image of a smiling, fair-haired young man appeared on the screen. She'd remember his face for as long as she lived. She'd watched him die, and it hadn't been from some airborne toxin.

Chapter 26

Lowell Stratford scrutinized Trina carefully as he watched her on one of the security monitors. He was sure her calm, cooperative demeanor boded well for the success of his plan. She voluntarily took a dose from her bottle of CSD then sat unblinking in her chair until Kevin entered the room and stood over her. He spoke as though he knew he would be obeyed without question. "Madalyn always gets your help, but today she can wait. Come with me."

Trina stood and followed him out of the room like a dutiful child toddling after her parent.

Power is a heady thing. Stratford chuckled and clicked his remote to check on the morning happenings in the employee break room.

8:49 AM

"I need about twenty minutes," Trina muttered as she followed Kevin down the hall, one pace behind him.

Kevin nodded, and they moved off in different directions. He went to his office and left the door ajar so he could keep an eye on the hallway that led to the secure ward. He paced nervously inside the tiny space, biting his nails, for what seemed like a million years but was actually more like seven minutes. Then he heard voices and hurried into the hall.

"Can't you keep track of your catatonic assistant? Using her was your idea in the first place."

Madalyn's voice was shrill. "It's not my fault. She wasn't in her office when I went to get her. How am I supposed to know where she went?"

Kevin skidded to a stop. "Hi, Madalyn! Trina's cleaning up the lab. She should be back here in about ten minutes. I told her she had to be done by nine fifteen."

"Oh. Well, I need her now. Go get her."

Kevin gulped. *Gotta stall for time.* "Hey, what's in there, anyway? I never knew we used this part of the building." He craned his neck to see past Stratford, who was standing in the open doorway to the secure ward.

Stratford waved him off. "Nothing that pertains to you." He started to close the door, but Kevin darted through.

"Hey! Cool..." He put his hands in his pockets and started down the hall.

"Come back here!" Stratford's voice sounded more surprised than angry, and Kevin quickened his pace. He didn't have much of a head start, and it was awkward trying to put some distance between him and the others without seeming to hurry. He glanced around, feigning interest in the space as he approached the room that held Sid Friedman.

"There's nothing to see." Stratford's legs were longer, and he was closing in fast.

Just before he got close enough to look in the window, Stratford overtook him and grabbed him by the arm. Still Kevin tried to stall for time. "Is this part of OCSD?"

"Yes, but this corridor connects to another building; we've kept it locked for security reasons." Stratford's smile was meant to be reassuring, but it was as terrifying as if he'd bared his teeth. He turned around, drawing Kevin with him, and something slammed against the door from the inside. Stratford jumped and hustled Kevin away, but not before he caught a glimpse of Sid Friedman's tattooed face at the observation window.

9:08 AM

Trina keyed into Stratford's office and used a paper clip to pick the lock on his drawer. She laid the presentation case on the desk and looked at the three unlabeled bottles of God-only-knew-what. *Time to stop that sonofabitch from taking over the world.*

Stratford's bottle was sure to contain the placebo. With shaking hands, she traded the bottle under the presidential seal for the one in the OCSD director's slot and slid the case back in the desk drawer.

She was sure Stratford planned to give Phase Three to the president and the chief quadrant marshal and make them his puppets. She smiled grimly. *Now Stratford will be the puppet. And I'll be holding the strings.*

6:36 PM

Trina turned on the desk lamp in her lab and powered up her computer. Stratford and Madalyn had spent the day ordering her around like she was some kind of Phase Two flunky who couldn't think for herself. She was sure they didn't suspect her of faking. Though she was playing her part well, she was running out of time to help the Resistance. She hunched over her computer keyboard, eyes burning from the long work hours and the glare of the monitor. She didn't know how to change the production sequence codes because there were just too many variables, but she was sure this week's production run was Phase Three, the formula even more potent and debilitating than Phase Two.

Her train of thought derailed as Kevin burst through the door. "Madalyn's still here! She's coming. Just saw her." She gritted her teeth. Of course Madalyn was still here. They'd be starting the new production run in a few minutes. *Maybe...maybe there was something that would work in time.* Her fingers moved rapidly as she fought to overcome her latest distraction before it was too late. Kevin pulled up a chair next to her and steeled himself for whatever was coming next.

She hit Enter with a flourish just a split second before Madalyn opened the door. *It's a damn shame there's no time for a high-five.* She settled for a surreptitious wink.

Chapter 27

Tommy woke at dusk, ate, and got ready to go out, just as he had the night before, but this time Careen was ready. She followed him into the night, and though she stayed just a few paces behind him, he never acknowledged her presence. Eventually, they blended into the crowd.

Most of the houses they passed were dark or dimly lit, but the high school stadium's lights shone so brightly that they seemed to beckon all the participants in from the streets. Tommy filed into the stadium with everyone else, but Careen slipped under the bleachers, where she crouched in the deepening shadows, out of sight.

Hundreds of people gathered on the football field and stood at attention. No one moved until soldiers with megaphones took their places on the sidelines and began the warm-up exercises. Everyone moved in perfect synchronization, like automatons controlled by one mind.

Soon the soldiers divided everyone into smaller groups. Tommy's group began with sprints on the track. After a precisely timed interval, the soldiers barked into their megaphones and each group marched parade-like to its next station. Careen strained to keep an eye on Tommy as he moved out onto the grass.

His new station was hand-to-hand combat. Tommy and his sparring partner punched, gouged, and kicked each other, leaving her horrified at the vicious energy with which they fought. In fact, all the people in training seemed eager to hurt their opponents. They also seemed oblivious to pain, because no one dropped out of the exercises or asked for medical attention. She couldn't bear to watch anymore, but as she plotted how to edge out from beneath the bleachers unseen, two soldiers patrolling the perimeter stopped right in front of her. She froze and held her breath.

"At this rate, we should have them combat ready in less than a week, sir."

"And how are things progressing in the other quadrants?"

"The same, sir. The national participation average is around eighty-nine percent. Those who failed to report are being located and detained." The rest of their conversation was lost in the crunch of gravel as they continued their march around the track.

Careen waited until their boots had completely disappeared from view, then made her way toward the concession stand behind the bleachers.

I'm supposed to be out there on that field. I've got to get out of here before someone sees me and makes me join in. She shuddered. *I wouldn't last two seconds.* As she hurried out of the stadium and blended into the shadows, she couldn't shake the feeling that someone was watching her.

Though she found her way home easily this time, she was even more frightened than she had been the night before. She carefully scanned the area around Tommy's house for signs of surveillance before she approached. When she was sure the coast was clear, she ran full-out across the lawn, bounded up the steps, and flew across the porch to her one safe haven.

Inside, she leaned against the door. *I feel every bit like the fugitive I am.* Her mouth was dry and she was exhausted, but she had work to do. *I'm going to need a little leverage to manage Tommy.* She rummaged in her messenger bag for the screwdriver she'd found in the kitchen junk drawer, then went upstairs and unscrewed the lockset on his door, turning the knob around so it could be locked from the outside. Then she returned downstairs and foraged in the kitchen through their ever-diminishing food supply. Plate in hand, she curled up on the living room sofa to watch PeopleCam while she ate.

There was nothing on the late news about people being forced to attend combat-training programs in quadrants across the country. She wasn't the least bit surprised.

Bored with the evening's programming, Careen tried to fall asleep on the sofa, but even with the drapes closed she felt exposed. She dragged the blanket around her shoulders, climbed the stairs, and burrowed under the quilt on Tommy's bed.

Chapter 28

Careen woke when the screen door banged shut. She waited until she heard Tommy start the shower before rolling out of bed. When she returned to his room ten minutes later, he was slowly pulling a t-shirt over his head, and she caught a glimpse of an assortment of bruises on his back, some purplish, others fading to shades of yellow and green. He straightened his shirt and turned around.

"Are you hungry?" She tried to keep smiling, but his face was so cut and bruised that her expression quickly became sympathetic. He didn't appear to notice. He shook his head wearily and sagged onto the foot of the bed.

She sat down beside him and touched his shoulder. "Tommy, do you know where you were last night?"

"Football. Told you." His voice sounded far away.

"No, I followed you, and it wasn't football. You really don't remember?"

"Mmmm…" He flopped back on the bed. She leaned over him, poking and prodding to keep him awake. "Listen to me. You can't take any more doses. No matter what. I know it hurts, but you *can't.* Do you understand?"

He snored. She sighed and brushed the damp hair off his forehead, and resolved to try again later.

11:08 AM

Careen sat cross-legged beside Tommy, whose legs still hung over the edge of the bed, toes just brushing the floor. She was amazed that he could sleep so soundly in such an awkward position. She smiled down at him. *I miss you. Hurry and wake up; there's all this stuff I need to talk over with you.* Elbows on knees, she put her chin on her hands and waited.

But when he finally came to, it was not the gentle Tommy who greeted her. He sat up with a roar and doubled over, clutching his stomach. She made a feeble attempt to soothe him, but it was definitely not a well-received gesture. He flung her aside with intimidating physical strength, and she tumbled off the side of the bed.

Undaunted, she chose the best weapon in her arsenal and aggressively locked her lips on his, hoping to distract him. Again, he hurled her away, snatched his sweatshirt off the floor, and clawed at the pocket for the amber bottle, but found nothing. His rage erupted, and he charged across the room, sweeping everything off his desktop before turning toward her. "Where is it? What did you do with it?" He took a menacing step toward her and she fled, pulling the door shut and locking it from the outside. A second later he hit the door like a freight train running full-steam, and his fury flared with the realization that she'd locked him in. Careen held the doorknob in a death grip as he battled to pull the door from its frame.

She called to him above the din. "I have to lock you in, but I won't leave you, okay? I promise. Count on it."

He let go of the doorknob and she listened as he pulled open drawers and flung things against the walls in a frenzied search for his CSD. She sank to the floor and leaned her head wearily against the battered door to wait for the storm on the other side to subside.

After a time she heard him retching in his bathroom, and the sound of running water. For a while there was a silence, which worried her almost as much as the turbulence had before, but then she heard him slide down the door and sit, just inches away. His muffled sobs pained her—but not enough to make her let him out. Not yet. She pressed her palm against the door for a moment and traced a heart with her finger. Then she rolled her eyes, annoyed by how easily she allowed herself to become distracted. She needed to focus on the business at hand; the other...stuff...would have to wait.

"Tommy? Will you listen to me now? I have so much to tell you, and none of it's good."

He sighed. "Yeah. Hit me."

She snorted without humor. "I think you've had enough of that. You've been in a kind of military boot camp thing for two nights now.

Tracy Lawson | 128

I followed you and watched what was happening. There were a couple hundred people there, and you all acted like robots. No one showed any fear, no one backed down even if they were hurt. It was so scary, Tommy. I heard a soldier saying you'd all be combat ready in less than a week."

He didn't answer, so she pressed on.

"And that's not all. They're arresting everyone who hasn't reported for training, so they're probably looking for me."

She felt the vibrations as he thumped his against the other side of the door. "We've got to get out of here."

"And go where? Even if we had someplace to hide, we don't have any way to get out. I wish I had a better plan, but I'm afraid you'll have to keep going to training and act like you're on your dose. Play along like nothing's different." *I don't know if he can do it without a dose. I couldn't.*

He grunted. She waited, and his silence encouraged her to continue. "Monday night I watched two quadrant marshals kill a guy who was running away from the training, but on PeopleCam they said he'd died from the poison. Tommy, they could kill us and lie about it, too."

More silence. "Someone was sneaking around outside the house on Monday night. I don't know what he saw, but if he knows I'm here, you'll be in trouble for letting me stay. I'm a fugitive."

"You're staying with me. I'll protect you. But what happens when I'm...combat ready?"

A lump formed in her throat. "I don't know. We'll have to figure something out before then." She pressed her forehead against the door and closed her eyes. "Tommy?"

"Yeah?"

"May I come in?"

"Count on it."

Careen unlocked the door, and the last barrier between them was gone. Tommy hauled himself to his feet as she came into the room. She smiled up at him, and caught his swollen hand in hers. Palms pressed together, she tenderly laced her fingers through his bruised and battered ones. "I've been waiting for you."

"Same." He pressed her against the door as he kissed her, and she basked in the familiar scent of his skin and the warm pink glow from the sunlight that flooded the room. His lips were gentle, and she responded in kind, conscious of his cuts and bruises.

She unfolded her fingers and stretched them, matching each of her fingertips to Tommy's. He pressed her hand against the door above her head, then trailed his fingers down her arm to the neck of her sweater. He pulled it back and bent close to nuzzle softly at her collarbone.

"Am I being too familiar?" His lips tickled as he spoke against her skin.

"No."

He reached under her sweater and encircled her tiny waist with both hands, his thumbs and fingertips nearly meeting as he squeezed. "Now?"

"Not yet..." Her arms went around his neck, and she pulled his mouth back down to hers.

He tugged the hem of her tank out of the waistband of her jeans, found her bare skin and slowly slid his hands upward. Her nerves tingled and she felt oh-so-pleasant goose bumps in the wake of his fingers.

She ran her hands up his back and raised his shirt over his head. He clawed it the rest of the way off and emerged in time to watch her strip off her sweater. She launched herself into his arms.

"Hey, watch it! I'm wounded, remember?" He laughed even as he winced. She smiled wickedly, and he murmured, "Just say the word if you want me to stop."

1:10 PM

Wes Carraway shrugged into his coat, picked up his Diet Coke, and headed for the door. He'd been reading procedure manuals all morning, and if he didn't get some fresh air soon, he'd go crazy. Henry Nelson was on duty at the front desk, pecking at his tablet, taking a statement from an impeccably dressed middle-aged man with crisp gray hair and a neatly trimmed moustache.

"I witnessed a young woman running away from training exercises last night. I came to file a report. It's my civic duty, you know."

Thank God for tattletales. Oh hey! I know that guy. He swung around and set the soda can down. "Mr. Severson? Wes Carraway."

"Ah yes, Marshal Carraway. Good to see you again."

Carraway jerked his head at Nelson, hoping he'd get out of the chair. "Nelson, I can take this report."

"Nah, it's okay. I got it." Nelson pointedly turned back to Severson. "Do you know her name, sir?"

Wes leaned against the wall, listening.

"No, I do not."

"Can you give me a description?"

"Not really. It was very dark, you know."

Nelson sighed. "That's not much to go on."

"Oh, but I can tell you where to find her. When I saw her leaving, I followed her. She went to my friend Tom Bailey's house and let herself in. Tommy, his boy, was at training at the time. I'm not sure why she failed to participate in the exercises like everyone else." He recited Tommy's address. "Remember, Carraway? We were all there together just the other day."

Wes nodded, but Nelson cleared his throat pointedly. "Thank you, Mr. Severson. I'll look into it right away." He smiled and took a long swig of Carraway's lukewarm Diet Coke.

Chapter 29

Tommy, drowsing in the afterglow of intimacy, lay with Careen's head pillowed on his shoulder, all his aches and bruises forgotten. Her fingers played in his chest hair, sending thrills through his body.

"I think I could count them. What, there's maybe thirty? Forty?"

"Ha."

He felt her smile against his shoulder. "You don't know the exact number?"

"Ha ha." He tickled her and she laughed. Really laughed. It was like music and hope all rolled into one, and he had to join in. *Happy. This is what it feels like to be happy. I'd forgotten.*

She propped herself up on one elbow and began counting. He lay back, perfectly content to let her.

"Forty-seven! I stand corrected. Wait…there's a couple more. Right. Over. Here…" She walked her fingers across his chest.

At that moment, the bedroom door burst open with enough force to leave a sizeable dent as it slammed into the wall behind it. Startled by both the noise and the sudden recognition of the man it ushered in, Careen pulled the quilt close. Tommy sat up to shield her.

Carraway stood in the doorway and looked at them appraisingly. "You've got five minutes to get out here. I'll be waiting." He pulled the door closed and left them in stunned silence.

She whispered, "That's the marshal who's been following me. I've seen him at least twice before."

"He was the one who dosed me that day on the porch." Tommy could feel her trembling against his back. "I guess we'd better do what he says." He got up and dug through the wreck of his dresser drawers for a pair of jeans and layered on a thermal shirt and a sweater.

When he turned around, she was buckling her belt and tucking in her tank top. "Hey," she said, twisting nervously at her sweater.

"Yeah?"

She seemed shy all of sudden. "I want you to know that…this…I really, you know, meant it."

He swept her into a strong, reassuring embrace. "Me too." He smiled down at her. "I'm still not sure how you found me, but I'm glad you did." He didn't want to let her go. Ever. "Now, come on. Everything'll be okay if we stick together, right?"

She nodded and took his hand, but as she stepped into the hall, Carraway wrenched her out of Tommy's grasp and shoved her down the hall.

As Tommy tried to protest, Carraway turned and, with one quick right to the jaw, sent him reeling back into his bedroom. Carraway slammed the door, and before he could regain his balance, Tommy was locked in for the second time that day.

This time, he listened helplessly to Careen's screams as Carraway dragged her down the stairs.

Carraway pushed Careen down on the living room sofa and stood between her and the front door. She'd stopped yelling, but her breathing was short and panicked.

"So what's your story?" he asked harshly. "Terrorist? Spy? Double agent?"

She covered her face with both hands and wept. He waited a bit and tried again. "Who do you work for? Whose side are you on?"

"I don't understand what you mean." She raised her head and looked at him accusingly. "All I know is you've been following me. I remember you."

He looked at her carefully. "Okay, let's take things in another direction. When—and why—did you stop taking CSD?"

"Friday. No wait, I mean Saturday. But I didn't stop on purpose! The sirens went off when I was here Friday morning, and I realized I was out of CSD. Tommy shared his last dose with me, and that afternoon the mailman walked right by and didn't deliver anything. It was late by then; we thought it was too late to get help. We thought we were going to die. We were too scared to go out and we waited…but we didn't. Die, that is."

"There's a warrant out for your arrest. According to our data, you've only taken your CSD twice in the last two weeks. How do you explain that?"

She grabbed at the chain around her neck and held up the vial. "I don't know, but I was taking my doses. I kept my CSD in here so I wouldn't lose it. I took it until I ran out on Friday."

He watched her carefully as she spoke, and he believed her.

Now that she was talking, she couldn't seem to stop. "Why didn't we die? Do we really even need to take an antidote? When Tommy and I ran out of CSD we...well, it took a day or so, but we went back to normal. I don't remember many details before then, but that's the point, isn't it? Everyone is sedated. Are we even in danger from poison at all? Why have you been following me? And what's the deal with the not-so-subliminal mind control stuff this week?"

Carraway chuckled, but his expression was grim. "You figure out all this on your own since Saturday?"

"Sort of, but I have a lot more questions." She sat up straighter. "I want my life back. So does Tommy."

"Your lives are mine, for a while at least. After that, I can't make any promises. But first I need to have a chat with him."

When Tommy heard the doorknob rattle, he flung the door wide and tackled Carraway low, driving him back into the hallway.

They grappled for a few seconds, and Tommy got in two solid punches before Carraway slammed him against the opposite wall, pinning him with a forearm to the throat.

"Hang on a second, will ya? I need to talk to you." Carraway fought to catch his breath.

"Where's Careen?" Tommy struggled to break free.

"She's downstairs waiting. She's fine, honest. I need to talk to you now—alone."

Tommy stared at him for a few seconds, and then relaxed as Carraway released him. "How long have you been clean?"

He shrugged. "Today."

Carraway stepped into Tommy's bedroom and grinned when he eyed the chaotic scene. "Withdrawal from Phase Two is hell, huh?"

"Yeah." Tommy was wary of the friendly shift in the marshal's demeanor. *So now he wants to be buddies or something? Right.* Carraway sat on the edge of the rumpled bed. "It's like that on purpose. It keeps everyone wanting their next dose."

Tommy sat on the window seat. "Careen locked me in here to get me under control. Otherwise I'd be..." He waved his hands in the air.

"Yeah. Hey, about that—I didn't expect to walk in on—well, you know. But if you'd taken your dose today, you would've been out cold. Then I heard voices and..." Carraway shook his head. "I know these questions are awkward, but about Careen—how long have you known her? What is she to you?"

Tommy rubbed his sweaty palms on his jeans. "Uhh...I met her for the first time last Friday. She's my friend and, well, more. Obviously." It was embarrassing being interrogated about his personal life, but he didn't seem to have a choice at the moment.

"Are either of you involved in any terrorist activity?"

"Hell no!"

"Has she said anything to you about being connected to the Resistance?"

"No. What does that even mean?"

"You don't know anything about the Resistance?"

He shrugged.

Carraway eyed him suspiciously. "You've never heard *anything* about the Resistance: people who believe the OCSD's safety policies are nothing more than a way to frighten, subjugate, and control the masses? People who've stopped taking CSD?"

"There are other people who stopped? Where?"

"All over, actually. I'm surprised you don't know anything about the Resistance. It's been around for a while. But there's plenty of time to fill you in on all that. First I need to tell you about your folks, Tommy."

"My parents?" Tommy was dazed by this rapid change of direction.

"Yes. The Resistance has located them."

"Huh?"

"They're alive. We're sure of it. We know where they're being held, and the Resistance has a plan to break in and rescue them."

Tommy nearly fell off the window seat.

Carraway looked at him soberly. "Your accident... well, it wasn't exactly an accident, if you get my drift."

"I never saw their bodies. Never got to say goodbye," he whispered, more to himself than to Carraway. "They held the funeral while I was in the hospital."

"Your dad was pretty well-connected in political circles and very vocal about his opposition to the OCSD and its policies. He had enough influence that the OCSD felt it was necessary to silence him. But I bet

Stratford wanted to pick his brain for information about what his home-grown enemies were up to."

Tommy shut his eyes for a moment to let it all sink in. "How do you know all this? Are you supposed to stop these Resistance people from rescuing my mom and dad?"

"I know about the plan because I'm part of the Resistance, too. Believe me, I know about your dad. His articles were required reading at my house when I was growing up. I can't believe he managed to keep you completely unaware of what he was doing. But as you can see, it's dangerous to oppose the powers that be. A bunch of the people who were reportedly killed by the toxins were also critics of the OCSD, and God only knows what really happened to them. Other members of the Resistance have been arrested or just disappeared. Now we know where some of them are being held prisoner, and we're going to do our best to get them back.

"I hope this is the last time I have to apologize to you. I'm real sorry I had to dose you on Monday. The order went out to find after your first bottle of Phase Two didn't get delivered, and I was trying to keep tabs on you and find Careen at the same time. She was on our watch list for making contact with a known terrorist, and then again for failing to take her CSD. I was watching her because I couldn't figure out if she was trying to join the Resistance or spy on it. Two different informants told us she was here, that she was buddying up to you. I hurried to get here today before another QM beat me to it. I have to keep up appearances when I'm at work, but I'm on the right side, Tommy. The side that's going to fix this mess."

2:26 PM

Tommy led the way downstairs. He spoke quietly to Careen, even though he could hardly contain his excitement. "He says my parents are alive."

"What?"

"I know! I can't believe it. We're going with him to help rescue them."

Carraway cut in. "Okay, you two. We're going to have to work fast and help each other out. Careen, you're a fugitive, and Tommy will be, too, when he fails to report for training tonight. I can get you away from here and out of immediate danger, but you have to trust me. Once we're on the road, I'll give you all the details. Got it?"

He nodded; she followed suit, although a bit more hesitantly.

"Where does your dad keep his computer, his work stuff?"

Tommy gestured down the hall.

Once in the office, Carraway began riffling through the contents of the desk drawers. When Tommy began to protest, Carraway held up a hand to silence him. "Try and find your dad's laptop. Any chip drives or hard copy files. Does he have a safe?"

"His laptop's missing. That's weird. I could've sworn it was here. What, exactly, are we looking for?" Tommy opened the bottom doors of the printer stand.

"Just told you."

Careen addressed Carraway, eyes narrowed. "Are we looking for...answers?"

"Yeah. Of course. I mean, any of his notes or files could give us answers."

"Shouldn't we just go rescue him and Mrs. Bailey? Can't you clue us in on your plan? I'd like some answers myself."

Carraway came around the desk and stood nose-to-nose with her. "Did you ever think that maybe you don't need all the answers?" She showed no signs of backing down, but before Tommy could intervene, Carraway's phone beeped. He glanced at the message with an annoyed expression. "Be right back."

Careen whispered, "I don't know if we should trust him. What did he tell you?"

Tommy shut the cabinet doors and quickly pulled an old hardback book off an upper shelf. He turned away from her as he flipped through the pages. "I didn't understand half of it. He says he's part of a Resistance group or something, and my parents were kidnapped because my dad wrote some stuff against the OCSD." He was reluctant to tell Careen she'd been on the watch list for associating with a terrorist. He wanted to see how she would react to the rest of what Carraway had said before he sprung that on her.

She frowned. "I'm certain he's the marshal who was following me. And he arrested a guy I know—for no reason! Why would he be targeting both of us? And what does he want from your dad's files?"

"I don't know, but the most important thing is to get my parents back. If we tick him off, he might not help us rescue them." He replaced the book then led her down the hall.

"Exactly where are we going?" Careen asked as she slipped into the warm plaid jacket he offered her.

Carraway came back inside, another marshal on his heels. "Headquarters," he answered. "You're both under arrest."

Tommy was too stunned to protest when Carraway handcuffed them and led them out the door.

Chapter 30

Tommy sat in the back seat of Carraway's patrol car, thinking fast as he tried to process this most recent turn of events. *Was he telling me the truth about Mom and Dad, or was it just a trick to get me to turn Careen in? She can't be a spy; that's completely ridiculous.* The whole Resistance thing was confusing. *Why had his dad concealed that side of himself?* He leaned close to Careen and whispered, "Maybe he told us the truth, and this is just part of the plan."

"I don't know. It looks like we're going to end up in jail." Careen paused. "But even that might be better than being...combat ready."

He grabbed her hand, and they rode the rest of the way in silence, their white-knuckled fingers entwined. He couldn't believe that just an hour before he'd been entwined with her in a completely different way.

At headquarters they were fingerprinted and photographed, then placed in separate holding cells. There was no chance to talk. No opportunity to say goodbye.

Tommy paced like a caged lion, wholeheartedly regretting the decision to put his trust in Wes Carraway. He was still fuming when the marshal came back four hours later, a Diet Coke in his hand. As he approached the cell door, Tommy reached through the bars and made a grab for his jacket. He missed, but hit the soda can and spilled it all over the floor. "I think you owe me another apology," he said.

Carraway grinned. "Whatever. Let's go." He took Tommy by the arm and steered him out the rear of the building into the cold night air, where he saw with relief that Careen was also being escorted to a waiting van. Carraway slid open the side door and steadied Careen while she stepped in, then pushed Tommy in after. The driver looked back over his shoulder, and Tommy couldn't believe his eyes. "Wait a second! You're the mailman!" He turned to Carraway. "What the hell is going on? Is this some kind of joke? He's the one who walked right by us and never delivered..."

"It's okay, kid. Eduardo's one of us. At least he is now."

Eduardo put the van in gear and pulled out of the parking lot. Once they were on the main road, Carraway removed their handcuffs.

"We can talk freely while we travel. That eager beaver Nelson showed up to arrest you, and I had to go along so no one at the station would get suspicious. Now I'm transporting two prisoners, and that's all they need to know."

The rutted road was riddled with potholes, and they hung on for dear life as Eduardo worked the wheel right and left to avoid them. "What's the deal with the Resistance?" Careen asked.

"Let me give you some background. After 9/11 and the terrorist attacks that followed it, the president issued an Executive Order to create the Office of Civilian Safety and Defense. Its original purpose in 2019 was to augment the efforts of Homeland Security and the old TSA. Since then OSHA and other organizations have been absorbed under the umbrella of OCSD. Anything that has to do with maintaining safety and security now falls under its purview, and it pretty much gets the last word on policy decisions. Lowell Stratford has more power than the president.

"The OCSD has been chipping away at our freedoms for most of our lives, all in the name of safety. But over controlling something doesn't necessarily make it safer or better, even though people don't realize it. They believe the OCSD keeps them safe and has their best interests at heart, but most of the OCSD's policies do more harm than good.

"OCSD pushed for the switch to debit cards, claiming it would be easier to track anyone who purchased items that went into the making of bombs or other weapons. But now they can monitor everything you buy, and where you bought it. You bought pastries and coffee at the bakery on Sunday, didn't you, Careen?

"OCSD said we needed to restrict travel and be selective about who could own cars so that they could better monitor people's activities and be on the watch for terrorist movement. But that keeps most people from visiting relatives or friends who live far away, or taking vacation trips. These decisions made in the name of safety have really messed up our economy because they limit what people have the ability to buy, sell, and offer as services.

"Every time the OCSD makes a new rule, it reminds us that the changes are a small price to pay for our safety. This happened gradually; people were so freaked out by the threat of terrorism that they either didn't notice or didn't care that their liberties were being stripped, one by one.

"Free thinkers, like those of us in the Resistance, want to decide for ourselves what's good for us. We'd like our private affairs to remain private. We'd like the chance to take a risk or even to fail occasionally. Because that's part of life.

"Tommy, your dad was the voice of reason for those who opposed the OCSD's actions in those early years. He reminded politicians about their responsibility to uphold the ideals that made our country great, but most of them ended up going along with the herd rather than risking a loss at election time.

"The worse things got, the more vocal your dad became. About a year ago, he got wind of Stratford's latest brainchild—a plan Stratford claimed would end terrorist attacks on our country once and for all.

"Your dad found out what Stratford had in mind, but before he could go public with the information, there was a tragic car accident. Your parents were reported killed. You were seriously injured, and the whole thing was hushed up so well that no one in the media bothered to investigate further. You were quietly given the best possible care then sent home.

"Three months later, the OCSD announced a terrifying threat against our country. No one was exempt from taking CSD, but I know people who were suspicious of the whole thing, never took a single dose, and survived every so-called chemical attack. Others who were hard-core or stupid enough to publicly refuse CSD mysteriously disappeared. Some of them were later found dead, supposedly from the effects of the poison. Right now, we know where at least five people are being held against their will, and we're going to get them out."

Careen couldn't believe what she was hearing. "Out of where?"

"OCSD Headquarters."

Everyone grew quiet as the night wore on. Careen fell asleep, and Carraway spent much of the time sending and receiving messages on his phone.

Tommy tried to rest, but he couldn't stop thinking about his parents and how much he wanted to see them again. A couple times he had to fight back the tears; fear, uncertainty, and hope made it nearly impossible to stay in control of his emotions. It was even harder to make sense of his current situation.

Tommy looked down at Careen as she slept, her head pillowed on his leg. With a lock of her silky hair gently feathering through his fingers, he dared, just for a minute, to imagine he could have everything he wanted.

Chapter 31

9:08 AM
Day 21: Thursday, November 16, 2034
Quadrant DC-001

Kevin planned to spend the day laying low in his office. Madalyn had commandeered Trina, giving him no chance to make contact with her and find out what, if anything, she'd been able to accomplish.

He heard the familiar ping of an incoming message on his computer and opened the document. A blanket of dread threatened to smother him as he read: by order of the director, he was being granted vacation leave until further notice. Effective immediately.

Before he could gather his thoughts, two security guards were at his door. They took his ID badge and escorted him from the building.

Kevin sat in his car, shaking, and fired off a text to Jeff: I blew it. Boss suspicious. They took my ID and escorted me out. Not sure if goal was accomplished or not. Security extra tight. Live presidential press conference on site 3 PM.

The response came back quickly: En route with backup. First priority find and extract. Press conference = intriguing possibilities. Where can we meet?

Kevin directed Carraway to the parking lot of an abandoned office tower a few blocks from the OCSD building and said he'd meet him there.

12:45 PM

While he waited at the meeting point, Kevin tried to control the swarm of thoughts that buzzed through his head. *Wish I could talk to Trina and find out what was going on.*

A black van pulled in and parked behind him. Kevin eyed the van warily until the passenger-side door opened and his contact stepped out. "Hey, Kevin."

"Jeff." He got out of his car and they shook hands.

The van's side door slid open. "Jeff? Who's Jeff?" asked a young woman from inside. Wes Carraway turned around, exasperated.

"Oh, come on. Just because we're the Resistance doesn't mean we don't have a sense of humor. We use code names, all right? I'm Jeff— short for Jefferson. As in Thomas."

Kevin peered into the van. "Seriously? Where's the backup? All I see is a couple kids."

"And a mailman," Tommy said, pointing at Eduardo.

Kevin fought off the sudden, overwhelming urge to puke. "Do you have any idea what security is like when both the director and the president are in the building?"

Carraway nodded. "That's why we're going to create a diversion over here. Divide and conquer."

A door clanked closed behind them. The janitor Kevin recognized from the OCSD sauntered out of the abandoned office building, clapped Carraway on the shoulder, and winked as he handed an OCSD identification badge to Kevin. "All access backstage pass, my man."

"Ready?" Carraway grinned.

"Oh yeah! We're ready." They all watched as the cocky janitor walked away, whistling and playing a one-man game of catch with what looked like a remote control device.

"I haven't seen him around the office lately," Kevin spoke mostly to himself.

"Oh, dude, that guy's not *really* a janitor. He's more of a pyrotechnics expert. Among other things." Carraway smiled in anticipation. "Just wait until you see his work."

1:24 PM

Careen stood outside the van, hugging herself against the cold air and fighting down her rising panic. Of course she wanted Tommy to find his parents, but she had a bad feeling about their part in the plan. She was convinced Carraway didn't care about her or Tommy. If they got caught in OCSD headquarters, he'd probably blame the whole thing on them. Even if they did succeed, they'd still be fugitives when it was over. She glanced over at Tommy. *I can't even think about what'll happen to us if we get caught.*

Carraway tapped Careen's shoulder, startling her. "Here's a lunch packet. And I brought a couple of these along for fun. A souvenir of your trip to the capital." He handed her a white paper bag and a black hooded sweatshirt bearing Sid Friedman's face and the familiar martyr slogan.

She hadn't realized she was hungry, but her stomach growled in response to the thought of food. She wasn't amused by the sweatshirt but slipped it on anyway.

After she ate, Careen strolled toward the side of the building and was momentarily distracted by the glint of a collection of discarded spray paint cans strewn haphazardly about.

One was neon pink. She smiled as she picked it up and shook it. There was some left in the can. *I like this souvenir better.* She took it back to the van and slipped it into her bag.

2:09 PM

Kevin led the way to the employee lot behind the OCSD building with the rest of the group in tow. He swiped the new ID badge at a side door, and the motley quintet slipped inside unnoticed and hurried downstairs to the secure ward. They followed Kevin down the dimly-lit hall to the door where he'd seen the martyr. Kevin peeked in the observation window. "Hey...wait a minute!"

The room was empty. He ran to the next door. That room was vacant, too. Tommy zigzagged the length of the hall, peering into one empty room after another. "You said they were here!"

"They were! I swear, I saw them yesterday." Kevin swallowed hard. *Now what?*

2:15 PM

Lowell Stratford escorted Hoyt Garrick, the chief quadrant marshal, into his office and poured him a drink. As Stratford extended the glass, he was belted by the shock waves from a nearby blast, the echoing booms assaulting his eardrums and threatening to shatter the office windows. Ribbons of red, white and blue fireworks erupted from a cloud of smoke a few blocks to the south. Garrick chugged down his drink and made a hasty exit for the scene of the blast. Within seconds, similar pyrotechnic displays began from adjacent rooftops, spreading out like ripples in a pond. Black soot rained down in the fiery aftermath.

Madalyn burst into the room. "Sir! Is it a terrorist attack? Shall we go someplace safer? Should I postpone the press conference?"

He turned from the window. "No, we're not going to postpone! Everything's already set up here. Get the situation under control, and whatever happens, do not let any of the news crews leave this building. Nothing must be allowed to detract from this press conference. The president is on his way, and between you and me, I think he's getting suspicious. He's been asking too many questions about how we're going to bring an end to terrorism, so the sooner we get him on his Phase Three dose, the better. Oh, and Garrick's on his way to the explosion site, so get Jacobs ready to stand in for him at the press conference."

"Her? Why not me?"

"She was the other doctor on the team. I'd prefer that she take the empty place."

Madalyn left in a huff. *Passed over for such an important national television appearance? Really? Well, this is the last time I'm taking a back seat to Trina Jacobs.* She went to the lab and pulled Trina's failed experimental batch of CSD from the refrigerator.

"I notice he's left me to get things under control. Again. This was the best the other doctor on the team could do, and yet she gets all the glory. I'm so sick of Jacobs this, Jacobs that." She filled a little amber bottle and slipped it into her pocket.

Chapter 32

2:43 PM

"I've got the bomber! I caught him!" Carraway shouted as he dragged Eduardo into the front lobby of the OCSD. Eduardo giggled uncontrollably. As they approached the security stand, Carraway flashed his badge and lowered his voice. "This guy's crazy. Do you have a safe place to hold him until after the press conference?"

The pimply security guard behind the desk looked about sixteen years old. He nodded nervously and motioned toward the elevator, stepped in and pressed a button. Carraway kept a firm hold on Eduardo's arm as he steered him through the open doors. They wasted no time and rushed the guard as soon as the doors closed, pinning him against the back wall. Carraway pulled an amber bottle from his pocket and dosed the guard, who slumped limply to the floor. "I'm never leaving home without this stuff," Carraway said as he pocketed the bottle. "Poor sonofagun—he's not going to feel too hot when that dose wears off."

"What do you mean?"

"There's something in the dose that makes people feel sick. They think they're being affected by the poison, and it scares them into taking more. Nice touch, huh?"

Eduardo shook his head in disbelief.

Kevin watched from around the corner as the elevator rose rapidly to the fourth floor, then led Tommy and Careen through a fire door and into an enclosed stairwell. They hurried up the first flight of stairs, but then he shushed them, and they tiptoed past the second floor. "The press conference is going to be in the atrium right through there," he whispered. There would be lots of reporters and OCSD employees milling about, preparing for the president's arrival, and he made sure they kept to the back hallways and out of sight as he hustled them along to meet Carraway and Eduardo.

2:44 PM

Dr. Stratford allowed himself one last glance in the mirror, then crossed the room and held the door open for Trina. "Davies, you bring the presentation case." He took Trina by the arm and headed down the hall. *Strange to see her so docile. And quiet. I could get used to this.*

Madalyn quickly switched the bottle in her pocket for one of the three already in the white velvet case before she hurried after them.

2:48 PM

The security guard, now glassy-eyed and compliant, led the way to a conference room at the end of the hall. Kevin, Tommy, and Careen caught up with the others just as the guard unlocked the door. Carraway glanced down at his name badge. "Larrison, return to your post. Forget this ever happened." The guard marched off toward the elevator.

Inside, three people lay restrained on hospital beds, parked around the outside of the long conference table.

Tommy held his breath while Eduardo approached the nearest bed. The large man under the blankets turned his head and everyone recognized the tattoo—it was Sid Friedman, the martyr. Eduardo undid the restraints and helped him sit up.

Tommy felt a surge of hope. He ran across the room and bent over the occupants of the other two hospital beds. He whirled around. "These aren't my parents!"

2:59 PM

Trina stood next to the president of the United States, her hands folded demurely in front of her, her expression blank.

The PeopleCam producer counted down. "And we're live in five...four...three..."

Trina slowly turned her head to look past the president. *Oh, Lordy, how I want to wipe that smug look off Stratford's face.* He caught her looking at him, and without thinking, she winked.

Stratford jerked like he'd been shot.

Oh no oh no oh no! Stupid stupid stupid... Trina's face was a mask of calm, but inside, she was in full-blown panic mode.

The president began to speak. "My fellow Americans..."

3:00 PM

Tommy advanced on Kevin, eyes narrowed. "My parents are Tom and Lara Bailey. You told Carraway they were here, and we drove all night to rescue them. So where are they?"

"I don't know. I didn't expect this to happen." Kevin backed away.

Tommy turned his fury toward Carraway. "What the hell? Now what do we do? Search this place room by room? You got another diversion up your sleeve?"

Carraway's bravado was gone. "Shit if I know. Roll with it." He shook his head. "Go search. Take Kevin with you and stay in touch. We'll get these three out. Meet us at the van as soon as you can."

Tommy risked a quick peek into the hallway and found the coast clear. He grabbed Kevin by the arm and dragged him out of the room without even a glance in Careen's direction.

He and Kevin searched every room on the top floor of the OCSD building, but saw no one. Tommy paused at the head of the stairwell. "I want to bust into that press conference and ask Stratford what he's done with my parents. Carraway said my dad was well-known. Maybe people will remember him and realize what Stratford's been doing, and what he's capable of. Maybe someone will believe the truth." He reached for the doorknob, but Kevin put a restraining hand on his arm.

"You can't help your parents if you're arrested. If you go in there, no one will side with you. Most of them are drugged and have no idea what's going on. Anyone who is aware will be too afraid to intervene. I was afraid, too. Now I'm just trying to be smart. Come on, let's check the third floor."

3:03 PM

The instant Tommy was gone, Careen wished she'd gone with him, but she pushed the thought away. This was no time to be clingy or weak.

She got Kevin's phone number from Carraway and added him to her contacts. "What's the plan?"

"Let's corral these three and take them to the press conference," Carraway said. "Nothing like a little show-and-tell, huh?"

She nodded in agreement. Bringing them in for all the reporters to see might force Stratford to admit the truth. Sid Friedman was able to stand and walk, and seemed remarkably together for someone who'd been held prisoner for nearly a month.

Careen was curious. "So what's your real story? You know you got a hero's funeral and all, for being the first casualty of this terrorist attack."

"Yeah? I'm on sweatshirts, too, from what I see."

"Oh, and posters. Lots of posters."

"How about that. Why do they call me a martyr?"

"They use you as a figurehead for CSD compliance. The OCSD said you didn't take your dose and you died from the poison."

"Huh. Well, it didn't seem to matter if I took it or not. The CSD didn't affect me much, even when I was here under lock and key. I didn't intend to become a poster child for CSD compliance or anything else. I was on the way to meet my son that morning. I'm not gonna lie— I wasn't the best dad. Hadn't seen him in years, and he'd agreed to meet me for coffee. I was almost there when the sirens went off. Everyone around me panicked, and I got so pissed. Why that day, of all days? I guess I went a little crazy. Next thing I knew I turned a corner and bam! I ran into a squad of QMs who knocked me out and brought me in."

"Wait...your son? On PeopleCam they said you didn't have any family!"

"Yeah, well, they got a lot wrong, didn't they? They had a fifty-fifty shot on whether I was alive or dead, and they blew that one, too."

"Let's go." Carraway cradled an emaciated older woman in his arms. Eduardo supported the other prisoner, a gray-haired man with thick glasses and a potbelly, and helped him walk slowly across the room. When they were all out, Careen closed the conference room door and followed Carraway toward the stairwell. It was slow going down the two flights of stairs. Once Eduardo stumbled, and it was Sid Friedman who steadied him. Carraway hesitated on the landing above the second floor atrium and shook his head. "This isn't going to work. We'll never get in and out of the press conference with these two being so weak and helpless. We'd better just go to the van."

"What? No! You're giving up, just when you have a chance to show everyone in the whole country that they're being lied to?" Careen couldn't believe her ears.

"This is not giving up. This is living to fight another day. We still have to get out of here in one piece." He and Eduardo continued down the stairs with the two prisoners.

"You're quite the motivational speaker until you're in danger yourself, you coward," Careen muttered as she watched them leave. Then she turned to Sid Friedman. "How would *you* like to create a diversion?"

He grinned. "Lead the way. I got nothing better to do today."

Chapter 33

Stratford stood at the president's right hand as he concluded his speech, but he was barely listening. *Trina played me for a fool. How long had she been pretending to take her CSD?*

"...and now, we must recognize with gratitude the individual efforts of Dr. Lowell Stratford, who was responsible for the development of CSD. With this ceremonial dose, we begin what Dr. Stratford refers to as Phase Three, in which he assures us, my fellow Americans, that we will work together as a whole to eradicate the threat of terrorism against our nation."

There was polite applause from the press corps and OCSD employees gathered in the atrium. Stratford, convinced Trina had planned some sort of sabotage, stepped in front of the presentation case with his back to the camera and switched his vial and the president's. He turned around with the case in hand, his smile a fragile façade as he struggled to mask the unfamiliar surge of panic that threatened to give him away. Cameras flashed.

Abruptly, a voice rang out above the dwindling applause and the murmur of the crowd. Neon-pink streaks glowed in the speaker's hair as she climbed on a chair in the back of the room. "I used to think that one person couldn't change anything. But now I see that isn't true." The crowd strained to locate the source of the interruption, and Stratford watched in dismay as they turned away from him.

"I want everyone to know the truth: this terrorist threat is a hoax! We don't need CSD. In fact, it makes us blind to what's going on around us. It can make us lazy and complacent—and it can also make us do things we wouldn't...shouldn't do."

"Ridiculous." Dr. Stratford's voice was calm. "Have her removed, please." The OCSD security team started toward her.

The buzz of conversation in the room swelled as the press corps shifted focus and formed a tight semicircle around her, cameras rolling.

As the security guards fought their way through the reporters and their equipment, a close-up of her face appeared on the screens located around the atrium.

"The OCSD is lying to us, manipulating us, trying to control us!"

The sound on the televisions in the atrium was muted, but everyone heard her voice, loud and clear.

The young woman held her ground on the makeshift dais, brave and defiant, as the security guards pushed through the crowd. Although her pink highlights and oversized sweatshirt gave her a childish appearance, her belief in herself and her message was evident in the self-assured lift of her chin. She pointed to her martyr sweatshirt and addressed the reporters gathered around her.

"Sid Friedman's funeral was mandatory programming. I must've watched it, like, five times that day. You all reported what you thought was the truth—that Sid Friedman died because he didn't take his dose. Everyone accepted him as a martyr. But he's not even dead!"

She pointed across the room. Sid Friedman stood up proudly and the crowd gasped.

Two security guards broke through the circle, dragged her off the chair, and forced her through the crowd of reporters. Sid Friedman shoved people aside in an attempt to help her, but more guards surrounded him and pushed them both toward the stairs.

"Ladies and gentlemen, your attention please!" Dr. Stratford smiled as though he didn't have a care in the world. "Let's carry on, shall we?"

As he looked to his left, his smile faltered. Trina was nowhere to be seen.

3:39 PM

As the press corps refocused their attention and their cameras on the front of the room, the president turned to Madalyn. "Where did Dr. Jacobs go?"

For once she had no clue how to respond.

"Won't you join us as our third then, Ms. Davies? For the official photos?"

She blanched, but stepped up beside the president and took the third bottle.

"Ready?" Dr. Stratford held up his bottle, and the others followed suit, cameras clicking and flashing as they raised the bottles in a toast. They twisted off the caps and squeezed the droppers. The president smiled at Dr. Stratford as they took their doses in unison. As Madalyn belatedly lifted her dropper, a strangled gasp broke the silence. She watched as a body crashed, lifeless, to the floor beside her.

Chapter 34

3:41 PM

As Tommy led the way down from the third floor, he heard the door on the landing below them click shut, and one set of footsteps on the stairs. Kevin motioned for him to stop. "Trina?" he called softly.

An attractive black woman glanced up and sagged with relief against the railing as they hurried down to her. "Kevin! Did you see what happened? We gotta get out of here! Some girl brought that martyr guy, the one with the sun tattoo, to the press conference and called the terrorist threat a hoax—in front of everyone! I ran for it when no one was looking."

Tommy went cold. "What happened then? What did she do?"

Trina must have assumed that if Tommy was with Kevin, he was on their side. "I don't know. Stratford told security to remove her, and that's when I got out of there. I had to scrap my plan. Stratford knows I'm not a good little worker bee. I couldn't help it, Kevin. I let him know, at the last possible second, that I wasn't on his team. It won't be long until he has his gorillas looking for me."

Tommy's feet kept moving down the stairs, but his brain felt frozen as he tried to think what to do next. *Security has Careen. My parents are still missing. Where is Carraway, or even Eduardo, when I need them?*

3:40 PM

Madalyn dropped her bottle and sank to her knees beside Dr. Stratford. She took his pulse. He was dead. The crowd stood in stunned silence.

Hands shaking, she got to her feet. The president's well-trained security detail saw to his swift exit from the atrium, and Madalyn stood alone in the spotlight. Every eye in the room—and every camera—was on her. Suddenly, she had all the power she'd ever wanted.

"It was Dr. Trina Jacobs! She assassinated Dr. Stratford!!" Madalyn pointed toward the door. "She's one of the terrorists! Find her! Stop her before she escapes!"

3:45 PM

Careen's feet barely touched the ground as security manhandled her down the curved grand staircase and into the lobby. Sid Friedman was too large to be dragged, so five guards formed a wall behind him and pushed. Several photographers stood at the railing, cameras whirring.

As they entered the lobby, Careen caught a glimpse of herself, up close and personal, on every screen in the room. PeopleCam was replaying her speech. *It's kinda surreal, watching myself being surrounded by security while I'm...surrounded by security.* The guards rushed their captives toward a back entrance, and as they rounded a corner, they came face-to-face with Eduardo, a bandanna tied over his mouth and nose. As everyone pulled up in surprise, Sid Friedman took advantage of the distraction and rammed two of his guards into the wall. They slumped to the floor, momentarily dazed.

Careen had spied the weapon in Eduardo's hand. She ducked, pulled up her sweatshirt's hood, and shielded her face with her hands.

The security guards let go of Careen in a futile attempt to protect themselves from a face full of pepper spray. She took advantage of her freedom and slipped past Eduardo.

Outside, Careen ran across the parking lot toward the van, Friedman and Eduardo at her heels. Carraway was waiting with the motor running and the side door open. The other two prisoners were slumped lethargically in the rear seats, looking pale and disoriented.

"Hurry! Let's get out of here!" Wes shouted as they clambered aboard.

Only Careen hesitated. "What about Tommy?" She pointed toward the building.

He shook his head. "Too dangerous. Can't wait for him. Come on, Careen! Do you want to end up locked in the bowels of the OCSD...or worse?"

"Try to get Kevin on his phone and see where they are! They might be on their way out with Mr. and Mrs. Bailey."

Carraway growled impatiently as he pounded out a message to Kevin.

She refused to get in the van until they had an answer.

3:47 PM

Emergency sirens screeched inside the OCSD building. Tommy led Trina and Kevin out of the stairwell, all attempts at stealth abandoned in their headlong dash to Kevin's basement office, where they ducked inside and locked the door. "We're as safe in here as anywhere," Kevin whispered. He switched on his television. The scene on PeopleCam showed pandemonium in the atrium. Sheila Roth reported the story from the newsroom.

"OCSD Director Lowell Stratford was assassinated just minutes ago during a live press conference at the Office of Civilian Safety and Defense headquarters in the capital. Early reports from the scene suggest he ingested a poisoned dose of CSD. It has been speculated that the tainted dose could have been meant for either the president or the OCSD director."

They showed a clip of Madalyn shouting to the crowd, "It was Trina Jacobs! She assassinated Dr. Stratford! She's one of the terrorists! Find her before she escapes!"

Tommy looked at Trina who gaped, wide-eyed, at the screen.

Kevin touched her arm. "Trina?"

"I didn't kill him!" Then she gasped. "Oh, Lord! Maybe I did! I switched Stratford's bottle with the president's yesterday, but I didn't know one of them was poisoned! I thought Stratford was going to put the president on Phase Three, and I switched the bottles so Stratford would get that dose instead. I thought I could get him to confess right then and there, on PeopleCam, and make everyone see what's going on."

Kevin's phone beeped. He read the incoming message and keyed in a reply.

Tommy just stared at Trina. He couldn't think of anything to say.

Chapter 35

3:55 PM

Carraway read the response from Kevin. "Stratford's dead."

Careen took a step closer to the open door. "What? How? I just saw him ten minutes ago."

"Looks like he was impaled on his own sword, so to speak. Poisoned by a dose of CSD." He paused for effect. "It's a small price to pay for our safety."

No one laughed.

"But where's Tommy? Are they coming?"

"From what I can tell, they're hiding somewhere in the building with Trina Jacobs. She's the one who was helping Kevin, right? Apparently she's been accused of the murder." He shook his head. "Doesn't look good. Guess we'd better go. We've got Friedman and the others; that's enough for our purposes."

"No! Absolutely not! We have to help them." She looked pleadingly at Eduardo, who sat behind the wheel.

"Come on, *jefe*. We should at least try." Eduardo spoke encouragingly.

Carraway exploded. "The Resistance is bigger and more important than any one person, or any one person's parents, for that matter. Do you know what would happen if you were driving sixty miles an hour, and all of a sudden you shifted into reverse? If we get caught, that's what's gonna happen—to the whole Resistance movement. Come on, Careen!" He reached out and urgently gripped her arm, the look on his face hungry as he pulled her into the van. "Ditch the kid and come with me."

Her eyes grew wide as she yanked her arm free, realization dawning. Carraway silently cursed himself. *Oh man. Did I really say that out loud?*

She stripped off the sweatshirt and grabbed her coat and messenger bag from the back seat. "No way. I'm going to find Tommy. You're free to leave." She jumped out and slammed the door. Carraway motioned for Eduardo to go, but he felt like a world-class jerk when he saw Eduardo shoot an apologetic look to Careen as he put the van in gear.

4:01 PM

Kevin bit his nails and stared at the television while he and Tommy waited for a response from Carraway.

"Here at the PeopleCam studios in our nation's capital, we've received reports of mobs gathering outside distribution centers and quadrant marshal stations, demanding to know if their next bottles of CSD are tainted like the dose that killed OCSD director Lowell Stratford."

Kevin shook his head. "The people that are worried about their doses are all on the placebo."

"Wait…what do you mean, 'placebo'?"

"Government employees never took the real CSD. They got doses of sugar water, so they'd be able to function and keep doing their jobs. The people who are taking Phase Two are in no shape to think, let alone protest. They're completely defenseless until they detox."

Tommy felt dazed. "So you took the placebo? You don't even know what it's like to take CSD, do you?"

Kevin shook his head apologetically.

Tommy realized it wasn't fair to be angry at Kevin. But nothing about this was fair. He turned back to the monitor.

"A spokesman for the OCSD has warned that there is no efficient way to test the bottles that have already been shipped and are due to be distributed tomorrow."

Pete Sheridan elbowed Sheila Roth. "What are you going to do?"

"What do you mean, what am I going to do?" Sheila seemed thrown off balance by the ad-lib.

"Are you going to take your dose from this week's delivery even though it could be poisoned?"

With a sideways glance at Pete, Sheila looked back into the camera and read from the teleprompter. "Recently compiled surveys report that forty-nine percent of the population is afraid to take their new dose…and the other fifty-one percent is afraid not to." A facial tic pulled her trademark smile askew.

Kevin turned to Trina. "So exactly what *did* you do to the CSD run? You've panicked the whole country, and I think Sheila Roth just blew a circuit."

She sank into his office chair. "Not what they're saying, if that's what you mean. I couldn't do what your guy Jeff wanted, either. I didn't have time to figure out all the codes in the sequences. That night when Madalyn was coming down the hall, I had to hurry, and I did the only thing I could think of. I opened the placebo file and renamed it. I hit "save as" and renamed the placebo file over and over. Then I deleted all the other formulas in the queue. I have no idea if it worked, but if it did, the whole country could have a placebo dose tomorrow instead of Mind-Control-in-a-Bottle."

"There's a chance it didn't work. Or that Stratford caught it before the run and changed it back."

She nodded. "No way to know for sure."

Tommy finally broke into their conversation. "Umm, not to interrupt or anything, but I need to feel like I'm doing something. They're not looking for me...yet. If it turns out you can't come with me, maybe I can find them by myself. But please tell me what to do, or where to look."

Trina turned to Kevin. "What's he looking for?"

"My parents, Tom and Lara Bailey," Tommy said. "Stratford's been holding them prisoner here. At least, he was. Now he's dead and maybe there's no one left who knows where they are. I have to find them."

She nodded. "They were here. I saw them just a couple days ago. Your mama has the prettiest red hair, doesn't she?"

Tommy's stiff upper lip never wavered. "Yeah."

"Come with me."

Kevin blocked the door. "No way, Trina! You're not going out there."

4:02 PM

Madalyn dabbed her eyes with a handkerchief. Someone brought her a glass of water. Groups of OCSD employees and reporters stood around, talking excitedly over the emergency sirens, but no one spoke directly to her. Lowell's body lay on the floor at her feet, covered with a tablecloth.

She crossed the room to get farther away from him, and was surprised that her knees felt unsteady. She wobbled to a seat and slipped off her shoes. What did it matter now? No one was watching. *This was not supposed to happen. Not this way. But at least Trina will still take the fall for a murder.* Her phone rang.

"Yes, this is she. Yes, I'll hold for the president." She slipped her shoes back on and stood up while she waited for the call to go through. "Yes, Mr. President. Thank you, sir. Yes, we'll talk about the transition tomorrow. A press conference?" She eyed the disorder in front of her, but answered, "Yes, of course. We're still set up here in the atrium. I'll have my staff notify the news agencies to return once everything is back under control. Thank you, sir. Good-bye."

She disconnected the call, rapidly dialed another, and shouted into the receiver. "You need to find her and find her *now*. I mean it. What have you been doing, anyway?" She paused and lowered her voice a bit. "Trina Jacobs is a threat to national security and she *cannot* be allowed out of this building. Yes. Use deadly force."

I'll be damned if I'll let Trina ruin this for me.

Chapter 36

4:03 PM

Careen pulled a hat out of her messenger bag and tugged down over her ears as she ran. *It was so stupid to spray pink highlights in my hair! I wanted to make a bold, unforgettable statement, and now I'm as recognizable as Sid Friedman.*

She worried that she had no ID badge to access the building, but she only stood outside for a few seconds before the outer door opened. A group of reporters was on their way out, but none of them recognized her as she walked past them. It seemed strange that the main lobby was completely deserted. The wailing emergency sirens unnerved her and she wasn't sure where it was safe to go, so she ducked into the ladies' room off the lobby. She checked the mirror to make sure her pink highlights were completely hidden under her hat, then shut herself in a stall and sent a message to Kevin.

4:05 PM

With the emergency siren as their only cover, Trina swiped her ID badge, pressed her thumb to the reader, and hurried Tommy into her lab. He jumped, his eyes darting about as the room filled with the sound of plaintive voices crying out to Dr. Jacobs.

"Oh, thank goodness! Now I can have that ridiculous recording disconnected."

Kevin brought up the rear and shut the door behind them. His phone buzzed, and he opened the incoming message.

Trina woke up her computer and began typing rapidly. "Lucky for us, Stratford is—was, rather—a maniacal record keeper. He was using Phase Two CSD to coerce your dad to cooperate." She stopped typing and sighed, ashamed of what she had to tell him. "He was dosing your mom, then putting her through extended periods of withdrawal, holding back her dose to force your dad to tell him whatever it was he wanted to know."

"Why didn't he just dose my dad? He could've easily made him talk without torturing my mom." Tommy's anger welled up at the thought of his own painful withdrawal symptoms.

"I imagine Stratford was well aware of his options. He probably thought using your mom like that would hurt your dad the most."

Tommy looked at her in disbelief. "And you stood by and let him do it?"

She hung her head. "I'm so sorry. I was outnumbered, and I was afraid of what they would do to me." Then she looked him in the eye. "I'm done making excuses now. Stratford's dead, and if we move fast, we might be able to find something in his files before they freeze everything and appoint a new director." She resumed her frantic typing and pulled up a folder. "Let's see what he's got here."

As they gazed at the computer, the emergency sirens stopped, and it was ominously silent for a moment. Then a voice came over the loudspeakers. "Dr. Trina Jacobs...turn yourself in. All the exits are being watched. A room-by-room search is underway. You cannot escape."

They all looked up at the speaker in the ceiling.

"Quick! Give me your phone and I'll download these files to it." Trina snapped her fingers at Tommy.

He patted down his pockets. "I must've left it in the van."

Kevin gestured toward the door. "We've got to get out of here, Trina. Your office is going to be one of the first places they'll look!"

"Hang on! He needs these files, and I've gotta do it the old-fashioned way." She opened a drawer, pulled out a disc the size of a quarter and inserted it into her computer.

Kevin already had his hand on the doorknob. "Let's go to the secure ward. I don't think anyone knows about it but Stratford and Madalyn. Stratford told me it connects to the building next door. If that's true, maybe we could get out unnoticed."

"It's a long way from here."

Tommy spoke up. "Sounds like our best plan, though."

"Ok, let's go then!"

"Hang on. This download is taking forever."

"You two go on without me," Tommy volunteered. "I'll wait for the download and meet you there."

Kevin shook his head. "No way. We should stick together."

"Maybe we'll be less conspicuous if we're *not* together. Careen's waiting for us downstairs. Tell her you're on the way, and I'll meet you there in five minutes, tops."

Kevin handed Tommy the janitor's ID badge. "We'll have Trina's, so you take this one. But you don't have a phone, so be careful. We won't be able to stay in touch."

Tommy watched them leave, hoping he looked braver than he felt.

4:06 PM

Careen fidgeted restlessly inside the restroom stall. *I want to pace, but there's no room! I don't dare leave until I hear from Kevin, but what if the guards find me first?*

Her phone lit up as Kevin conveyed the news that they were on their way down.

She replied that she'd be ready.

She was poised to make a run for it, but froze with fear when the outer restroom door opened with a bang.

4:09 PM

Tommy turned off the lights while he waited for the file to download, listening with one ear for anyone milling about in the hall. He scrolled through the files in the folder and opened a few that looked promising, skimming the first few pages quickly. He wanted the information they contained.

The last download was nearly complete when he heard voices. He moved into the shadows of a corner behind the door just as someone entered the room.

"Help us, Dr. Jacobs! Save us, please!" The voices pleaded.

The security guard was momentarily distracted by the recorded voices, and Tommy took the opportunity to attack. He slammed the guard's face against the wall until blood spurted from his nose, then spun him around and pummeled his face with a right hook, a left, and a brutal uppercut to the chin. A couple hard punches to the torso, and the guard slid to the floor in agonizing defeat.

Tommy towered over him, breathing hard, rattled by what he had just done instinctually, automatically. *Could I have learned to fight like that in just two nights of combat training? If so, this guy would've been a better security guard if he were on Phase Two instead of the placebo.*

His jacket sleeves and the front of his sweater were splattered with blood, but that couldn't be helped. He removed the guard's handcuffs from his belt, secured his hands behind his back, and dragged him out of sight behind the desk. He smashed the guard's phone with his heel, and ejected the chip disc containing the downloaded files from the computer.

He cautiously opened the door a crack and peered out into the empty hallway. Someone was searching an office across the hall, two doors down, and Tommy didn't wait around to be found. He ran for the stairs and was halfway to the second floor before the hallway door closed behind him.

4:12 PM

Careen jumped when she heard the door open and peeked through the crack next to the stall's door. An older woman, part of the cleaning service, shuffled into the room, emptied the trash, and began to mop the floor.

Is it better to walk out like nothing's wrong or to try and hide? She took a deep breath. *Go for it.* She flushed the toilet and exited the stall, washed her hands unhurriedly, and was headed for the door when she noticed the older woman looking at her intently.

Then she heard a familiar voice outside the door. "Honey? Are you still in there?"

She shrugged at the woman and replied, "Coming, Dad!" and bounced out the door like she didn't have a care in the world.

She bumped into Kevin just outside the door, and they walked as nonchalantly as they could toward the stairwell. "I'm not exactly old enough to be your dad," he muttered.

They were almost to the door when someone shouted, "Hey! Hey, you!" from the second-story balcony.

Careen stiffened, but he whispered, "Just keep walking. Pretend you don't hear."

They pushed through the stairwell door, grabbed Trina and hurried to the basement.

4:12 PM

Tommy moved quickly, but quietly, after his initial dash into the stairwell. His whole body was pulsing with adrenaline and all his senses were on high alert, but a part of his brain was chewing on another thought. *There* was *a security guard who was on Phase Two. The guard Carraway dosed in the elevator. Larrison? Yeah, that was his name. Larrison knew where Stratford had moved the prisoners. Did he also know where they've taken Mom and Dad?*

He had to find Larrison. His leg began to throb in protest, and his shoulders sagged for a second, but he turned around and began to retrace his steps.

He crept out into the second floor atrium, aware that he was vulnerable in the open space, but he couldn't accomplish his goal by hiding. He noticed a guard across the room, looking down into the first floor lobby.

"Hey! Hey you!" Tommy yelled, and the guard turned around. It wasn't the right one. *I bet I could attract a couple more if I tried.* He tore across the atrium with the guard in hot pursuit and recklessly took the grand staircase three steps at a time. He picked up speed until he landed wrong on his right leg and it crumpled beneath him. He tumbled down the last few steps and was instantly back on his feet, oblivious to any pain, as he dashed through the main lobby past the security stand. No one was there. *Figures*, he thought as he ran.

An elevator door stood open, and Tommy had a good lead on the guard, so he jumped into the car and pushed the button for the basement level. The door slid closed, and he sagged against the wall.

Chapter 37

4:15 PM

Tommy shouldered his way out of the elevator as soon as the door opened and barreled around the corner, almost colliding with Kevin, Trina, and Careen. "Go! Go! Go! I don't know if he followed me!"

Together they ran to the door of the secure ward. Kevin swiped Trina's ID twice, but nothing happened. Tommy shoved him out of the way, and they all breathed a sigh of relief when the janitor's ID did the trick. No sooner were they inside then they heard footsteps in the hallway. "You must need special clearance to get in here. Maybe they don't have the right IDs," Kevin whispered.

They backed against the wall and stood motionless, barely risking a breath, as someone tried the door, zipped an ID card through the reader, and rattled the doorknob again.

"Larrison, come on! Nobody's in there."

Tommy could barely contain his frustration. *The guard I need is two feet away.*

As soon as the sound of the guards' footsteps faded, Kevin motioned for them to follow him. Tommy drew Careen to his side and they whispered, heads close together, as they walked down the hall behind Trina and Kevin.

"Are you okay?" he asked. "I heard about the press conference. I'm sorry I wasn't there to protect you."

"It's all right. Eduardo had pepper spray. He helped me get away."

He looked around. "Where is Eduardo, anyway? And Carraway?"

"They left. Apparently Carraway decided your parents were not a priority. Neither were we," Careen said.

"Yeah. Not surprised. We're better off without him."

"But what about you? You're limping." She took his hand and noticed the blood on his cuff. "And you're all bloody!"

Tommy shrugged. "You should see the other guy."

She giggled softly, and he was glad he hadn't resisted the urge to joke. It felt good to break the tension, if only for a moment. They came upon a solid metal door at the end of the hall that looked like it belonged on some kind of vault. It had a card reader, though, and when Tommy swiped the ID, it clicked open. Careen shrank from the pitch-black darkness inside as Tommy peered past the door hoping for a view of something…*anything*. He shrugged, and Kevin and Trina exchanged a worried glance. No one was in a hurry to take the first step into the void. Tommy couldn't even tell if there was a floor.

"I could feel inside for a light switch," he said dubiously. *I can't quit now, but…*

"Wait!" Careen said, rummaging in her bag. "I brought this from your house in case I needed it." She held up a flashlight.

Tommy played the beam around the room and found a light switch on the wall. Even in the glare of the overhead light, Careen hung back, hesitant to step into the unfamiliar space.

Once they were all in, Kevin closed the door with a resounding clank, like the clatter of a rusty cell door locking into place. Tommy had the awful feeling that this room had been used for exactly that.

The space was empty except for a desk and a chair. Tommy pulled open one of the drawers, and something slid to the back. He reached in and found a bracelet made of antique gold chain and twisted strands of pearls, glass beads, and polished green agate stones, with a lock-and-key charm dangling near the clasp. He held the bracelet in his palm and lovingly traced the dainty strands with his finger, remembering. "This is my mom's; I'm sure of it. They were here."

He handed the bracelet to Careen and yanked open the other drawers, pulling them all the way out and turning them upside down in a desperate search for more hidden clues, but there was nothing else to find.

Meanwhile, Kevin and Trina inspected another door, opposite the one through which they'd entered. It was rusty but opened easily to reveal a staircase, lit with low-wattage emergency lights.

Kevin turned to Trina. "What building is this? What's next door to OCSD, anyway?"

"I'm not sure which side of the building we're on. I get disoriented when I'm inside."

"There's only one way to find out. Tommy, you and Careen wait here while we go figure out where we are."

As soon as they were alone, Tommy pulled Careen close, drawing strength from her embrace. "I can't stand the thought of my parents being locked up in here. How could I not have realized they were still alive?"

"You can't blame yourself for any of this. Let's concentrate on finding them."

"Thanks for being here. It wasn't even your fight."

"It is now."

He lifted her chin and pulled off her hat and smiled at the spray-painted highlights as he ran his fingers over her hair.

"We'll find your parents."

"I know. But first we have to find a security guard. Specifically, we have to find Larrison."

She frowned. "What for?"

He finished explaining just as Trina and Kevin returned.

"The stairs lead out to a parking garage. It's just getting dark outside, so we should be able to slip out, no problem. My car's in the employee lot around the corner." Kevin smiled for the first time since Tommy met him that morning.

"That's great. But we're not going with you."

"What?" Trina and Kevin cried out in unison.

After a brief explanation they agreed to Tommy's plan. "You two stay here until we message you that we made it out. Hurry and find Larrison, then meet us at the car." Kevin pulled the door closed behind them.

Tommy perched on the desk and drew Careen between his knees, then took the bracelet from her and fastened it on. He slipped two fingers between the bracelet and the inside of her wrist, and closed them around the lock-and-key charm.

"Gotcha." He looked at her for a long moment, and when he kissed her, it felt unhurried, as though they had a lifetime in front of them. "Here's what I know for sure," he said, planting gentle, heartfelt kisses on her eyelids, first one and then the other. "Everything's going to be okay. I'm gonna make it happen."

She opened her eyes. "I'm counting on it."

Chapter 38

4:31 PM

Kevin and Trina crept up the stairs for the second time and stepped cautiously into the parking garage. It was expansive, left over from the days when almost everyone owned a personal vehicle, but now there were only two cars and a mail truck in sight. Their footsteps echoed off the crumbling walls. He stopped for a moment to send the all-clear text to Careen, and then hurried to catch up with Trina. She hesitated at the low cement wall that bordered the parking garage. "Where's your car?" she whispered.

"In the back row." He pointed. There was open ground to cover between the garage and the OCSD parking lot, but there was no one in sight. The street lamps had just come on. "Ready?"

Before they could bolt, Kevin felt a heavy hand on his shoulder.

He whirled around and blindly threw the first punch of his entire life. It wasn't much of a blow, but he followed it up with a two-handed shove that knocked the surprised security guard off balance. Trina swung her legs over the low cement wall and took off across the grass and into the parking lot. He followed, but she was a faster runner, and he was about twenty yards behind her when a voice yelled, "Trina Jacobs, freeze!" from somewhere near the rear entrance to the building.

Kevin spied the second security guard, who stood silhouetted in the light from the street lamps, gun pointed at Trina. He watched what happened next as if in slow motion.

Trina hesitated and turned back toward the shelter of the parking garage. Tommy sprinted out the back door of the OCSD building. A single gunshot rang out just as Tommy hit the guard with a flying tackle, and Trina crumpled to the pavement.

As the world seemed to resume revolving at its normal speed, Kevin cried out in horror and ran to where Trina had fallen. Careen hurried out of the building to kneel with him at her side.

Tommy had Larrison pinned facedown to the sidewalk, but the guard seemed oblivious to any discomfort. "I got her! I got Trina. She's the terrorist!" he said softly.

Tommy rolled him over and straddled his chest. A surge of anger welled up in him, and his hands closed around the guard's throat. "Where are the other two prisoners?"

"Baileys…" Larrison's windpipe was so constricted that his response was a raspy whisper, barely audible.

Tommy loosened his grip a little. "Yes! Yes, the Baileys! Where are they? Are they here? Who has them?"

"Not here anymore. They left with Mr. Severson."

"Severson? Wait, not Art Severson?"

Larrison sighed and relaxed. "Yeah. That's him."

Tommy picked up Larrison's gun and, not sure what else to do with it, stuck it in the back of his waistband. He pointed a menacing finger in the guard's face. "Don't move. I mean it."

Tommy joined Kevin and Careen, who were frantically trying to stem the flow of blood from Trina's wounded arm. It had soaked the shredded sleeve of Trina's blouse, and Careen quickly pulled a scarf from her bag and applied a makeshift tourniquet. Trina cried out as Careen applied pressure to the wound.

"Where did you come from?" Kevin asked Tommy.

"We'd just opened the door to the lobby when Larrison ran past us, shouting that he'd found Trina. It was…well, it was just like in the movies. So we followed him."

Trina gritted her teeth as she tried to sit up, and clutched Tommy's arm. "Thank you."

He nodded. "We gotta get out of here. There are other guards looking for you. And I know who has my parents."

They all helped Trina to her feet, and she leaned on Kevin as Tommy and Careen ran ahead toward Kevin's car.

Before they were halfway there, a black sedan screeched across the parking lot, headlights blazing, and jerked to a sudden stop between them. A man dressed in dark clothing leaped from the back seat and pounced on Kevin and Trina, wrestling them into the vehicle. Before Tommy or Careen could react, the car swung around and was gone, tires squealing.

They stared at each other, completely at a loss. Without Kevin, they had no transportation.

"What'll we do now? We can't go back in there!" she cried. Before he could reply, a white postal truck swerved into the parking lot and screeched to a halt beside them. Eduardo rolled down the passenger side window and shouted, "Hey! Where you been? Hop in!"

They scrambled gratefully into the back.

"I ditched that idiot Carraway about ten minutes after we left you, Careen. Liberated a truck, just like my old one. I been waiting in the parking garage over there, trying to figure out what to do. I saw Kevin run past me, so I got out here as fast as I could. Where you wanna go?"

"Umm…follow that black car!" Careen pointed vaguely.

"Where? You see which way it went?"

Tommy shook his head. "No. No way. They're gone. We don't know which direction they went or who took them. Let's go home, regroup, and figure out how to find my parents."

She nodded reluctantly, then pulled out her phone and keyed in a message.

Tommy shut the door and sank back on the pile of mail bags, where he shifted uncomfortably. They were filled with little cardboard boxes. *Crazy. The safest I've felt in days is here, in a truck full of CSD.*

Careen frowned. "Kevin's not answering."

5:03 PM

Kevin and Trina sat silently in the back of the black car as the driver gunned the accelerator and flew up a freeway entrance ramp. Theirs was the only car on the road. Kevin's nerves were at the breaking point. He drew a shuddering breath, and immediately felt ashamed of himself for showing weakness. When Trina pressed her right hand over the wound in her left arm, he put his hand over hers gently. He heard his phone beep, but before he could reach for it, the man who had pushed them into the car turned around in the passenger seat. "I need your phones, please."

Kevin pulled his from his jacket pocket and handed it over without looking at the message.

Trina shook her head. "I don't have one."

The man accepted Kevin's, removed the battery and memory card and tossed the pieces out the car window, then spoke to them gravely.

"You realize your old lives are over. You can never go back to your jobs at the OCSD. You can't go home. Your employer will be looking for you, and they'll want to silence you. But you have new lives waiting and a chance to change the world—for good." He offered his hand to Kevin over the seat. "Welcome to the Resistance."

5:23 PM

It was nearly dark in the back of the mail truck, which Tommy hoped would downplay the bloodstains, bruises, and the half-healed cuts on his face. *I'm a mess. She looks...perfect.* Careen's skin was pale in the light from her phone, and the neon pink streaks in her hair gave off an eerie glow. They had hours and hours ahead of them before they reached home. "We got away."

"Yeah." She looked up at him and smiled.

Just then Eduardo turned the steering wheel hard, avoiding God-knows-what in the roadway. Tommy took full advantage of the momentum that threw him against Careen and tackled her, rolling her gently into the lumpy pile of mailbags. She wriggled into a hollow, seizing the lapels of his jacket to pull him in with her. *Damn. It hurts to kiss her.* He couldn't remember a time that it didn't hurt when he kissed her. But that didn't mean he was going to stop. Some minutes later, Tommy fumbled in his pocket and winked at Careen. She pushed him back a few inches and threw a meaningful glance at Eduardo.

Tommy stole one more kiss. "Where's your phone?"

"Huh? Why?"

He held up a chip drive. "Stratford's files. Trina pulled them up on the OCSD's main computer." She plucked the chip from his hand and closed her fist over it, grinning triumphantly.

Tommy sat up, dug into his left shoe and produced a second chip. "And I found this one in my dad's office."

"You hid it from Carraway?" She looked impressed.

"I wasn't giving him anything until I'd read it first. It's high time I got up to speed anyway."

They looked around for the phone, and when he saw the glow from the screen reflected against one of the canvas bags he rescued it and loaded the chip. If their kiss lingered longer than it took to bring up the files, he didn't notice. "We don't have to read it right this minute," he murmured against her hair.

"But we should."

He playfully held the phone out of her reach as he nibbled his way along her jaw and caught her earlobe lightly between his teeth.

"We should…" she protested halfheartedly. His free hand slid under her sweater and he felt her respond to his wandering fingers.

"We really should…" this time her voice was low and inviting. She rolled on top of him and parted his lips with her tongue, drawing him into the depths of the kiss. His brain checked out and the next thing he knew, he was pinned. By a girl. He didn't protest when she plucked the phone from his hand and tapped the screen to pull up the file. "See what the OCSD says about your dad first?" He nodded reluctantly. He'd been stalling, and not just because making out with her was fun; he was worried about what the files might contain. If he'd learned anything in the last twenty-four hours, it was that he knew almost nothing about his dad.

They stared at the screen, expecting the OCSD file to appear. Instead Pete Sheridan looked directly into the camera lens and cleared his throat.

"More mandatory programming," she gasped. "Oh no! What if they caught Trina and Kevin?"

"Just moments ago, Madalyn Davies was named the new director of the Office of Civilian Safety and Defense. She will assume immediately the post left vacant by the death of Dr. Lowell Stratford."

Tommy recoiled involuntarily when Madalyn's face appeared on the tiny screen. *Even at that size, she's intimidating.*

Madalyn stood at a podium with the OCSD seal behind her and addressed the camera. "Our country was prepared for this most recent terror attack because of the efforts of the late Dr. Lowell Stratford. Those who survived by taking CSD owe their lives to him. Now I call upon everyone to help bring Dr. Stratford's killer to justice.

My first act as director of the OCSD is to offer a five-million-dollar reward for information leading to the capture and conviction of the person responsible for his murder."

Tommy and Careen both gasped as a not-so-flattering photo of Trina flashed on the screen. Her hair was messy, her blouse askew, and her eyes unfocused. "How would anyone even recognize her from that picture?" he wondered aloud.

"Trina Jacobs, a disgruntled former employee of the OCSD, masterminded this terrorist attack and Dr. Stratford's murder. She took a co-worker hostage and was wounded in a shootout with a security guard as she made her escape late this afternoon. She is extremely dangerous. Anyone with knowledge of her whereabouts should call their local quadrant marshal station immediately. The terms of the reward also apply to this unidentified individual, thought to be Jacobs' accomplice in the assassination." The person of interest had neon pink streaks in her hair. Tommy swore as Careen dropped the phone and covered her mouth with both hands to stifle her scream.

For a long moment, neither one spoke. Then Careen lowered her shaking hands from her face, and an anguished flood of words burst forth. "This is crazy! I don't know anything about Stratford's murder! They're only after me because of what I said at the press conference. I never even met Trina until after Stratford was dead, but that won't matter. Oh! What'll they do when they catch me? Kill me? They've killed plenty of other people who didn't do anything wrong."

She paused for breath, and before she could gear up for more, Tommy pulled her into a tight hug and rocked her gently. "We'll be all right. We can handle this. Think about it. We've been in danger ever since we met."

Her laugh sounded more like a sob. "You keep saying 'we'. But it's me they're looking for. Not you."

"That doesn't matter. We're a team. They're looking for you because you put yourself on the line for me and my parents. I won't forget that, and I'm not leaving you. Ever." He kissed her fiercely. "We're still going to do exactly what we planned. You can count on it."

"But how? How will we rescue your parents if the quadrant marshals are after me?"

"The same way we would've before. We're getting pretty good at improvising. We just outsmarted those security guys, right? If Eduardo can get this truck going faster than thirty-five, we'll be miles away before the quadrant marshals get around to looking for you. They won't expect us to go after my parents, they'll expect us to hide. We'll find my folks and then go volunteer for the Resistance."

Eduardo pressed the accelerator in response.

She smiled, though her eyes still threatened to overflow with tears. "You'd be a lot safer without me, you know."

"Life without you?" Tommy shook his head. "That's too high a price to pay for my safety."

ACKNOWLEDGEMENTS

Chase Montana Smith, my collaborator and friend, whose well-timed writing prompt triggered the epic brainstorm session in which the idea for Counteract originated, is the best 'gresser' I know, and I thank him for creating the characters Tommy and Eduardo and then entrusting them to me.

Susan Hughes, my brilliant editor, caught my many grammatical errors and helped shape the final draft. I'm so glad she has my back.

Kathy Rausch, my wonderful web designer, made all my website wishes come true.

My nieces, Reagan, Madison, and Ainsley Stone and Alexandra and Jules Pearson, read drafts of the manuscript, asked questions that prompted blog posts, and cheered me to the finish line.

Dawn Wilson, my trainer, did beta-reader duty while I did planks and burpees.

Members of The Resistance Fan Club, who downloaded the first chapter and now get to read the rest of the story: Kristan, Larissa, Brandy, Tracy, Meg, Kate, Bob, Ian, Alex, Celia, Kory, Sycho, Amelia, Kathy, Dan, Duane, Marissa, Keri, Isaac, Kendall, Orianna, Tom, Elizabeth, Alice, Delaine, Sandi, Jim, Kim, William, Frances, Rhonda, John, Anne, Gary, Caleb, LauraLee, Julie, Micah, Emily, Mo, Sherri, Emily, Dawn, Job, Roxy, Jane, Tony, Jason, Todd, Susan, Rob, Rachel, Elias, Jessie, Michael, Therese, Landmere, Lorene, Jenny, Shelagh, Cookie, Zoe, Tommy, Melissa, Ananias, Hoyt, Casimira, Brad, Jeff, Cheryl, Marisa, Ave, Angela, and Janine. Thank you!

About the Author

Tracy Lawson has wanted to be a writer ever since she learned to read. She earned her Bachelor of Science in Communication from Ohio University, and though she embarked on a career in the performing arts as a dance instructor and choreographer, never lost her desire to write, and thus far has to her credit this first volume in a coming-of-age dystopian thriller series and an historical nonfiction. Her interest in writing for teens is sparked by all the wonderful young people in her life, including her daughter, Keri, a college sophomore.

Other Books by Tracy Lawson

Resist: Book Two of The Resistance Series

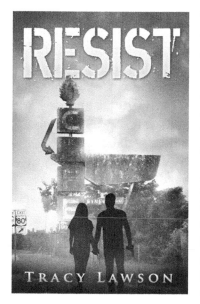

Tommy and Careen are no longer naïve teenagers who believe the Office of Civilian Safety and Defense can protect them from a terrorist's chemical weapons. After accidentally discovering the antidote's true purpose, they join the fight to undermine the OCSD's bid for total control of the population.

Being part of the Resistance brings with it a whole new set of challenges. Not everyone working for change proves trustworthy, and plans to spark a revolution go awry with consequences far beyond anything they bargained for. Tommy and Careen's differing viewpoints threaten to drive a wedge between them, and their budding relationship is tested as their destinies move toward an inevitable confrontation with the forces that terrorize the nation.

Bonus Excerpt from Resist: Book Two of the Resistance Series

After a while, Tommy grew more confident behind the wheel and actually enjoyed the drive to the lake. Most of the autumn color had faded to brown, but it was a crisp, sunny day, perfect for a drive in the country. This late in the season, the area was sure to be deserted, and he wished he were taking Careen to his family's old vacation spot under different circumstances. The private road was muddy and rutted, and Tommy slowed the car to a crawl. He parked above the lake, out of sight of the house, and led Careen through the woods toward the shore.

They paused in the cover of the trees and watched as a woman, wrapped against the chill in a fringed wool blanket, walked slowly along the beach. When she drew nearer, Tommy whispered, "That's my mom!" Before Careen could stop him, he dashed out of the woods.

Lara Bailey turned toward the sound of his footsteps, but when she saw him she backed away, pulling the blanket close.

Tommy kept advancing. "Mom? Mom—it's me!"

"I don't know you. And I don't have a son. Stay away from me!" She turned and hurried up the path to the house. "Art! Art…"

He ran after her and closed the distance between them easily. He took her by the arm just as Art Severson came out on the porch.

Tommy motioned him back into the house and guided his mom inside. Careen followed and closed the door behind her.

Art was pale, his clothing disheveled, perspiration beading on his forehead. "Get the hell out of here or you'll mess things up."

"I don't take orders from you. Where's my dad?" He lowered his voice. "Why doesn't she know who I am?"

Art smiled and inclined his head toward Tommy's mother. "We've been pretending like nothing's wrong," he said. "She doesn't remember what happened."

Up close, Tommy could see the glazed, faraway look in his mother's eyes. She obviously hadn't detoxed yet. *I hate that stuff.*

"Lara? Art? What's going on?" Tom Bailey came slowly in from the kitchen. He was much too thin and looked older and grayer than Tommy remembered. Their eyes met, and at first he thought his dad didn't recognize him either, but then he drew a long, sobbing breath and whispered, "Tommy?" He sagged against the wall and began to laugh weakly. "Tommy! Art, that's Tommy. He's alive!"

Tommy nodded, getting more annoyed by the minute. "He knows. I stayed at his place for two weeks after I got out of the hospital."

Lara looked from one to the other. "Tom? Who *is* this?"

Tom Bailey tried to compose himself. "I'll introduce you in a minute, honey. First, Art and I need to talk with this young man."

Tommy threw a quick look at Careen, and she gently took Lara's arm. As soon as the door closed behind them, Tommy advanced on Art. "Is the QM coming?" Art looked away. "How long before they get here?"

"Tommy, what do you mean you stayed with Art? Art, why didn't you tell me? How could you let me think he was dead?" His father was clearly trying to keep up.

"You have no idea what I've been up against." Art turned on Tommy, defiant and unapologetic, and Tommy felt a surge of rage. He pulled the gun and leveled it at Art's head.

His father tried to get between them. "Tommy, what's gotten into you? Art got us away from Stratford and brought us here where we'd be safe."

"Is that what he told you? Dad, get your stuff. And hurry. Please." When his father was out of earshot, he took a step closer to Art, eyes narrowed. "How could you let him think you'd rescued them when you're just babysitting until the quadrant marshals get here?"

"You have no right to judge me for anything I've done. You have no idea what was at stake."

"I'll judge all I want. You just better hope I don't get mad enough to shoot you."

"Oh yeah, tough guy? I'll tell you what happened, then you tell me whose fault this is. Your dad decides to singlehandedly take down the OCSD and Lowell Stratford. Me, I mind my own business. Then one day some of Stratford's goons come to me and say, 'Put a muzzle on your boy Tom Bailey.' But there's no stopping your dad once he gets started. Soon the goons are back on my ass, and this time it's, 'Gosh, you have a pretty wife. It'd be too bad if anything happened to her.' But I can't stop the great Tom Bailey—he's decided to expose Stratford's plan to fake a terrorist attack. Now don't get me wrong—I'm no fan of the guy myself. But why does your dad have to stick his neck out, especially when it's also my neck and Beth's on the line, too? But before he can blow the whistle, the creeps in the dark suits show up a third time and say, 'Congratulations, you're getting promoted at work. Invite the Baileys over for dinner to celebrate.' I ask what's going on. They say, 'Stratford's decided there needs to be an accident.'

"No, I say. There has to be another way. I'll do whatever you ask. So we make a deal. They agree to let your parents live if I agree to give them all your dad's files about Stratford.

"So Beth plans a big, fancy meal for the four of us, but your folks show up with you as a last-minute addition to the dinner party. You're a kid, and you're innocent, so while Beth's setting an extra place, I make a call and beg them to cancel the plan. But they won't. They say if I try to warn your dad, there'll be a home invasion robbery-turned-murder instead of just a little car accident.

"I'm sweating bullets, but by the end of the evening all I can say to your dad is 'Hey, drive safe on the way home.' Before long there's a call from the hospital. You survived, but you're badly hurt. You won't ever be the same again." He paused and fixed Tommy with a look that in the past would've made him squirm, but Tommy felt nothing but anger. Finally Art went on. "They won't tell me where Tom and Lara are. And it's *still* not over because I can't find the goddamn files. I turned your place upside down while you were in the hospital, and again while you were living at my house. I tried one last time, about two weeks ago, when you were outside in the yard. I got Tom's laptop, but there was nothing about Stratford on the hard drive.

"Last week, they tell me Tom's alive, but he's not cooperating. To motivate me—or maybe to punish me—they switched Beth's CSD dose and now she's checked out most of the time. They're watching everything I do and say. And that's the last thing I remember. I woke up here this morning. I'm out of the antidote, okay? And now I'm…" he turned and vomited onto the floor.

Tommy wrinkled his nose against the smell and was caught off guard when Art came up swinging. He ducked, but must've squeezed the trigger, because the gun went off with an ear-splitting bang, shattering a window pane. He was so freaked out by the way the gun had bucked in his hand that he threw it away and caught Art with a hard right to the jaw. The older man sank to his knees in the puddle of vomit. Tommy carefully retrieved the gun.

His dad stood in the hallway, staring at him, open-mouthed. Tommy wondered how much he'd overheard. "Dad?" He patted his father's bony shoulder. "Come on. We're outta here." He opened the door and saw Careen running up the path, a terrified look on her face. She skidded to a stop.

"I thought I heard…is everyone…still alive?"

"Yeah, no worries."

Art stumbled out the door after them, and pulled his phone out of his pocket. Tommy shook his head. "No phone privileges for you, mister. And no driving, either. Hand 'em over."

Art rolled his eyes as he tossed the phone and his keys to Tommy. Tommy tilted his head toward his parents and lowered his voice.

"Take them to the car, Careen. I'll be there in a minute."

Her eyes flicked between his face and the gun in his hand. "Don't you think you've made your point?"

"Just go. Everything's fine." When they were out of sight, Tommy walked Art over to the clump of trees near the beach. "You know, you do have a very pretty wife, and she deserves much better than a jerk like you. As for me, I'm not all that innocent anymore." He stared at Art coolly. *Let him wonder about that for a minute.* "Remember the combat training they made me take? I've found it comes in handy. The skills are applicable in almost any situation." He pointed the gun at Art's head.

Fips, Bots, Doggeries, and More: Explorations of Henry Rogers' 1838 Journal of Travel from Southwestern Ohio to New York City

Fips, Bots, Doggeries, and More (2012) is based on a journal written by Lawson's great-great-great grandfather, who kept an account of his family's 55-day journey on a horse-drawn wagon. His observations about the social and political environment of the times, emerging technology, and his family's health and comfort while on the road were all commented upon in the journal. After making most of the same trip herself by automobile--along with her young daughter--during the summers of 2003 and 2004, and keeping her own journal, Tracy was inspired to compare and share information about both trips--taken over a century and a half apart. Fips, Bots, Doggeries, and More won the Ohio Professional Writers Association's Best Non- fiction History award in 2012, and was featured in the Ohioana Book Festival in 2013.

Made in the USA
Middletown, DE
14 February 2019